a delicate dance of souls

karen d hamilton

a delicate dance of souls
Published by yes and also press, inc.
Centennial, CO

Names: Hamilton, Karen Diane, author.
Title: A delicate dance of souls. / Karen D. Hamilton.
Description: First trade paperback original edition. | Centennial [Colorado] : yes and also press, 2020. | Also available as an ebook.
Identifiers: ISBN 978-1-7341465-0-9
Subjects: LCSH: Veterans—Fiction. | Spirituality—New Age movement. | Man-woman relationships—Fiction.
BISAC: FICTION / Visionary & Metaphysical.
Classification: LCC PS374.L6 | DDC 813.6—dc22

Cover art by Janet Hamilton

QUANTITY PURCHASES: Companies, professional groups, clubs, and other organizations may qualify for special terms when ordering quantities of this title. For information, email karen@yesandalsopress.com.

This book is printed in the United States of America.

"In Karen D. Hamilton's tale of friendship and self-acceptance, the main characters must learn to trust others and to identify internal demons. ...Readers will steadfastly follow the characters' journey of self-discovery... Infused with spiritual lessons, this story about two lost souls finding their way back to themselves proves a satisfying read."

—BlueInk Review

"Matt and Nicole's sexual relationship is built upon mature expectations and open conversations... [that] involve psychological grappling: with the inner child, dark parts of the human psyche, and reconciling the past. ...[T]heir relationship is vulnerable and eye-opening."

—*Foreword* Clarion Reviews

"Karen D. Hamilton's first novel is all about the relationship challenges everyone faces. It takes us on a journey of profound insights through the eyes of her unique characters. As they are able to see past the limiting beliefs that formed the framework of their lives, we also can catch a glimpse of how we can see past our own limitations. A delicate dance of souls is an easy read that moves along. It was hard to put down."

—Norman Wolfe, author of *The Living Organization: Transforming Business To Create Extraordinary Results*

For Becky,
Cherish the Dance!
Karen

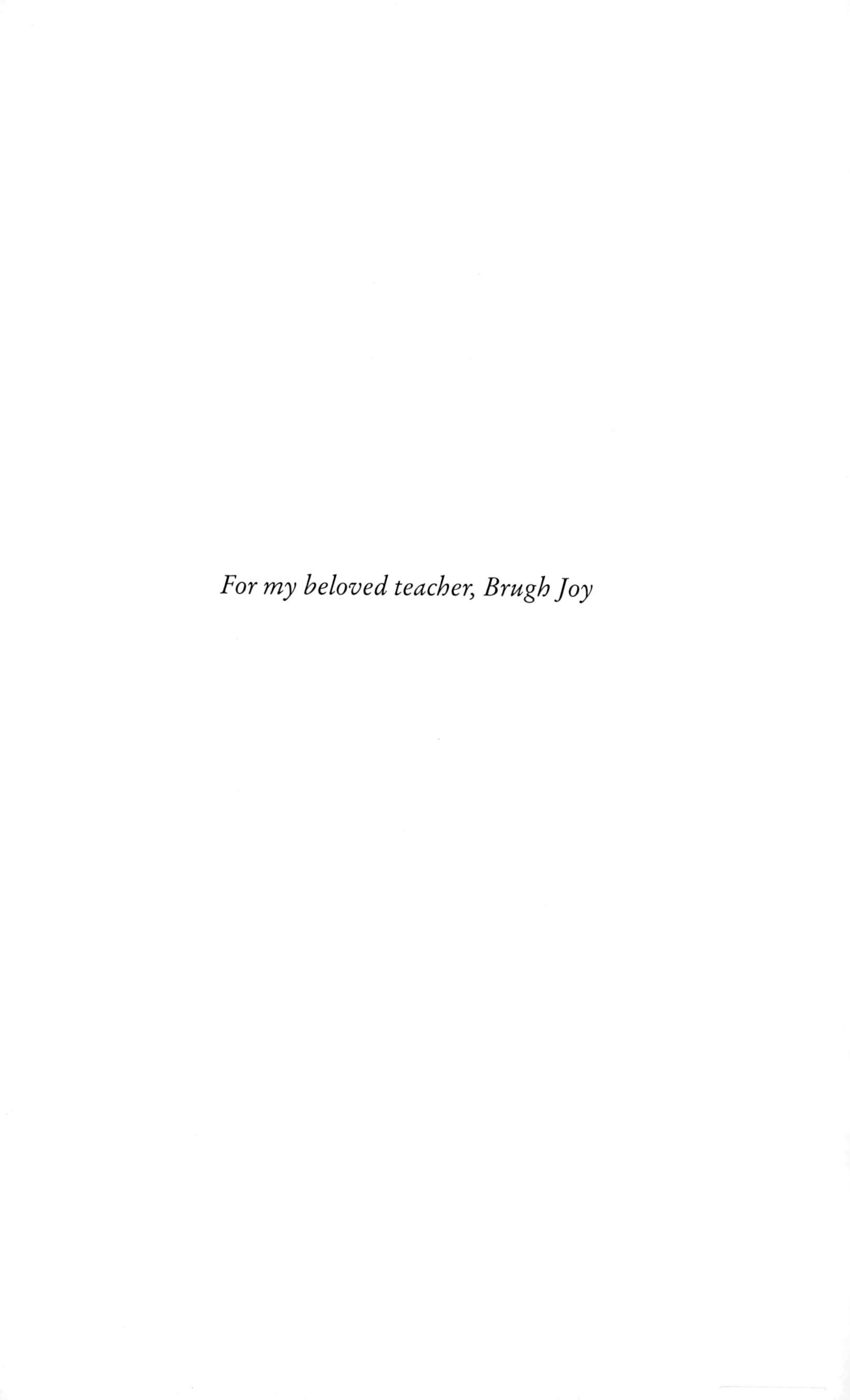

For my beloved teacher, Brugh Joy

chapter 1

Matt had just finished putting his sleeping bag and clothes into his tent and was walking back to the Jeep when he heard the music. His head turned toward the pop-up camper in the campsite closest to his. The sunlight shone brightly, like a spotlight really, onto the woman dancing inside. From where he stood, the music was faint, but clearly she could hear it, and feel it, for she danced as though there was nothing else in the world. He stood transfixed, watching her hips swaying seductively in surrender to the rhythm, her arms expressing the emotion of the song that commanded her. Through the screened window, it was all he could see of her, this vision, but the sensuality and love in the way she moved touched him deeply. And like a bolt of lightning, it reverberated through his whole being—*I have to know her.*

His marriage to the only woman he'd ever loved had broken up three years ago. Amanda had left him not long after his return from Iraq. He was not over it yet, probably would never be, and he certainly wasn't looking for a rebound relationship. He'd come here just looking for some peace, a respite from the pain and anguish of the last few years. But this woman, and the compelling flash he'd felt, was something separate from all that. A moment and connection suspended in time, not to be denied.

chapter 2

Nicole peeked out the camper window when she heard the Jeep go by. She'd been so enjoying the solitude since her friends had left earlier that day and was a bit disappointed when the Jeep backed into the campsite next to hers. *Ah, well, I guess I couldn't really expect to have the place all to myself.* She went back to the task at hand, rearranging everything in the camper for her week of meditation and reflection in the mountains.

While the others had been with her, she couldn't spread her things out as much, but now the camper was all hers, and she put everything out just as she liked it. Plastic storage bins with drawers held her clothes, and she put them at the end of the "couch," behind the slide-out benches. She could hang her shirts just above them on the pull-down rod. The coffeepot and toaster oven were already set up on the counter, but now there was room to set her books down too. She set her iPod and speakers on top of the bins, plugged them in (the campground had electricity, yay!), and turned on some tunes. She couldn't help but dance, and after a few songs, she decided it was happy hour.

She was standing at the back of her truck, getting ice out of the cooler for a drink—Long Island Iced Tea was her favorite for camping—when the man from the Jeep came up to her. The confident, graceful power in the way he walked, and his tight muscular body attracted her instantly. Surprisingly, she also sensed that this person was going to be important in her life.

"Hi, I'm Matt. I'm in the campsite next to yours. Just wanted to introduce myself."

He was immediately struck by her eyes as she turned toward him—deep blue, the same color as his. But unlike his, there was a soft kindness in them, and a wisdom born of experience. Looking into them, he suddenly felt like a warm blanket had been wrapped around him. Light brown hair, cut shoulder-length, fell in soft waves around her face. Her lips curled up slightly at the corners impishly, and when she smiled, her whole being seemed to invite him in. The connection he'd felt when he saw her dancing strengthened.

"Hi Matt, I'm Nicole. Nice to meet you." Her earlier thoughts about not wanting a neighbor disappeared as she looked more carefully at him—full but firm lips, longish, brown hair lying casually on his head, nicely tanned skin with about a two-day beard starting, and oh yes, those beautiful blue eyes. She liked him instantly.

"How long have you been up here?" he inquired.

"A couple days so far. I come up every year for a week. This place is so great, so peaceful. Feeds my soul."

"Yeah, I know what you mean. I just got here, but I can already tell it's impossible not to relax in these mountains. I've never been to Wyoming before, and I'm so glad I came. I really wish I could stay longer than just two days. I have to head back on Wednesday."

"I'm here till next Sunday." She peered into his eyes for a moment, felt his energy. *Yeah, I think this guy is okay, someone I'd like to know.* "Would you like to join me for a drink?"

"Um, sure. What do you have?"

"Well, I'm drinking a Long Island Iced Tea. I also have some wine, or a gin and tonic. Or I can make you a margarita. Any of those sound okay?"

"Wow, that's quite a few choices. Planning on partying a lot while you're here?" He had a boyish grin that made his eyes crinkle.

"I had some friends up over the weekend, and they left most of this. You're right though, I guess I am ready to party."

"All right then. I'll take a margarita, bartender," he said, grateful their encounter would continue.

While she fixed both their drinks, Matt watched her closely—her hips as she walked, her gentle hands as she poured the tequila. What was the word to describe her figure…voluptuous? Definitely not your high school virgin twig of a girl. No, this was a full-out *woman.* He felt that stirring below, the start of something he'd denied himself lately, yet here it was again. Surprisingly, it felt right, and good somehow. *Hey, you just met her. Cool it.*

He tossed those thoughts aside, and casually, he hoped, asked about her camper.

"Oh, it's really great, one of the best treats I ever gave to myself. Want to see inside?"

"You don't mind? I've just got a tent, and I've been thinking about upgrading."

"Come on." She gestured for him to join her.

They took their drinks inside, and Nicole showed him all the features of the camper she'd bought three years ago: the mini fridge, propane stove, sink that ran hot as well as cold water, the heater, the slide-out table, and benches. She'd made rugs for the floors—not so cold on bare feet in the middle of the night—and pillows for the couch. Miniature Coleman lantern LED lights hung all around the windows above the table and cabinets. She explained they gave a much softer light than the camper's overhead lights.

"If you get one of these, you have to get the slide-out," she told him. "It totally opens up the floor space. Makes it pretty roomy inside." She sipped her drink, enjoying the warm glow of the alcohol.

"Yeah, I can see that. And those beds are big too."

Just for a second, Matt flashed on how it might feel to be with her in one of those beds, and he blanched. Quickly, he turned to the table and tried to refocus on the camper's features. He breathed a small sigh of relief when Nicole continued her description in a casual tone.

"King size, both of them. These benches can be a bed too, when you put the table down," she said as she sat down.

He slid onto the bench across from her and took a slow sip of his drink as he looked around. "This is nice. I could see camping in this for a month, if I could get that kind of time off."

"So what kind of work do you do?" she asked, already feeling unusually drawn to him.

"I'm not really working full time just yet. I dropped out of college to join the Army, which is done now. I've got one more year to finish in school, and then I'll be teaching history, at the high school level, hopefully. How about you?"

"I started out as a psych major in college but wound up with a job at Cheyenne Frontier Days after I graduated and got hooked on event planning. Project work. I love the flexibility of that. I can take a job that goes for three months, then take a break before starting another one. It gives me a chance to travel, go camping. Though sometimes I just veg out in front of a bunch of movies."

Matt ran his fingers through his hair, and Nicole felt a rush of heat.

"Wow, that sounds great," he said. "I have to admit part of the attraction to teaching is the summers off. Well, mostly off. There's always planning and meetings in the summer, but a lot of free time too. What kind of events do you plan?"

"Mostly weddings, birthdays, big parties. Once in a while we get some corporate getaway where the bigwigs from the East want the 'Western experience.' My business partner Sam is a great chef, so he brings in a lot of that business."

He looked almost shy as he said, "So how come you're up here alone? No man in your life?"

"Nope. And not likely to be."

Matt blushed and squirmed in his seat. "Oh, sorry, are you gay?"

She laughed. "No, not gay. Just kind of sworn off serious relationships with men after my first marriage. Sam's been trying to convince me otherwise ever since we met. Long story."

"I got time..." He realized with amazement that he would be happy to hear anything she might want to say, no matter how mundane. Anything, as long as he could spend time with her, be near her.

She felt the longing, and a hint of an ache in his voice, considered, then said, "I was actually just about to heat up some stew for dinner. Want some?"

"Sure, that would be nice if you have enough. Can I help?"

"You may indeed." She smiled gaily as she stood up. The tone of his voice confirmed what she'd sensed—his need to be with her even though she didn't yet know why. And in that undercurrent, something in her reached out for him too.

They busied themselves with making dinner. She'd brought up several containers of stew and other dishes prepared at home, which were easily heated on either the stove or in the toaster oven. Corn seemed like a good complement to the stew, so she got some of that cooking too. Then she pointed Matt to the firewood, paper and matches to start a fire in the campsite pit. He looked so natural and competent while assembling everything for the perfect blaze that she stood and watched him from inside the camper while the food heated. He was clearly strong, and beautifully built with a round, firm butt and muscled arms. Not too muscled thankfully; she thought those extreme bodybuilder types were basically grotesque. She did like a man who was capable though. His hands grabbed the wood firmly, and he lifted the logs easily, but when he pulled the match out of the box, his fingers were delicate, deliberate, controlled. For a flash of a second, she could feel how they would be if they were touching her, and her blood flamed.

The stew bubbled, and she turned to concentrate on dishing up their plates, getting tableware, napkins, salt and pepper. When everything was ready, she brought it all out to the chairs set up by the firepit. They sat and admired the view of the tumbling river and rugged rock cliff beyond, and the fire now burning in earnest, then continued the conversation while they ate.

"Ready to tell me that story now?" Matt prompted.

"You sure you want to hear this?" she asked, surprised.

"Yeah, I actually do." He couldn't explain his profound desire to know more about this woman, but he couldn't deny it either.

"Well, okay then." Nicole sensed it was somehow important to fully open herself up to him in this moment. She took in a deep breath. "I married Jason in college. We'd had a bit of an on, off, on-again relationship. Went through that several times. And each time we were apart, we both went out with other people. I really wanted to just be with him—you know the whole marriage, kids, forever thing that all us girls are taught to want. And he kept saying that's what he wanted too, so when he proposed, I said yes. We had a fun wedding. My family meshed with his pretty well, and it seemed like a perfect match. But after a while, it became clear that he wasn't so committed as I'd thought."

"What happened? This stew is really good by the way." He had been eating heartily and was nearly done already, Nicole noticed.

"Oh, thanks. You know, at first it was little things. Flirting with other women and so on. Which I tried to ignore, or make excuses for. I really loved him and wanted the marriage to work. Know what I mean?"

"Oh, yeah, do I ever. One of my best buddies from college fell into that always making excuses thing. It was sad to watch."

Nicole seemed lost in contemplation for a minute and then scowled. "At one point, we became friends with another couple, Paul and Andrea, who kept talking about their open marriage. I certainly made it clear I never wanted an open marriage, but Jason actually looked interested. Then one night when Jason was out of town for some reason—I forget now—Paul called me up and asked if I needed anything. Even though I said no, he kept saying well he could come over and keep me company or whatever. It felt really strange, like he was pushing himself on me."

"So what did you do? Did you let him come over?" Matt was

intrigued.

"No, it took a lot of talking cause he kept insisting, but I finally said a firm no and hung up. I've wondered since if maybe Jason had encouraged that somehow, as a way to start a wife-swapping thing. Guess I'll never know for sure, but it just felt so contrived. About the same time, Jason got involved in a political campaign, and there was a meeting at our apartment for some of the volunteers. There was one cute young blonde that Jason just latched onto—flirting, showing off. It was so obvious I couldn't ignore it."

"He's starting to sound like a real jerk." Matt took a sip of his margarita and looked at her sympathetically.

"Well, he kind of was. Honestly, I don't know what he was thinking. I really started having doubts after what happened with another couple we knew, John and Susan. We'd been pretty close, doing all sorts of things together. They were a sweet couple, had this little Chihuahua dog that was really sweet too, not a yapper like so many are. Then one day, Jason mentioned he'd had lunch with Susan. They both worked downtown, and he'd asked if she wanted to get together. Suddenly she and John had a million excuses why they couldn't do things with us. It felt really strange to me, just being cut off like that. I ran into them about a month later. They were very friendly with me, but there was this look of pity on their faces, like they felt sorry for me. I can still feel that, how we said goodbye. Never saw them again."

Nicole slumped in her chair, remembering the pain of that creeping realization that something was really not right with her marriage.

Matt frowned. "That seems pretty strange. Almost makes you wonder if he made a pass at Susan when they had lunch."

"That's what I started thinking. But of course, I had no way to prove it, so I didn't think I could bring it up. And you know,

I still wanted to believe we had a good marriage and that he was committed to me. Then we moved to Denver, got in with a new bunch of friends. One night we were all hanging out at our house when Nancy, this woman Jason had flirted with, up and said, 'I know what we can do. Let's play hide and seek in the dark.' I had this instant image of Nancy and Jason hiding in the same closet making out. That was it. I was done."

That night had ended the marriage for her. Nicole sighed and shook her head.

"I never really told Jason why I wanted out, just said I did. He kept saying he didn't want to split up. Even his mom called and asked if I wanted her to pray for us. Sometimes I wonder if things could have been different if I'd told him my suspicions, confronted him with all of it. But deep down, I just felt that if he was so not committed to us through the first year and a half of our marriage, then talking about it wasn't going to do much good. So I left him, came back to Cheyenne." Her voice was resigned, but she shrugged and put her hands up in a "what you gonna do?" gesture.

Matt marveled at her openness, that she would reveal such deeply personal and obviously painful details about herself to him, a temporary interloper in her life.

"Good for you. I know I'm a guy, but I don't have much respect for men who don't honor their commitments. I'm guessing you got divorced," he said gently.

"Yes. And after we were done, he went back to a woman he'd been engaged to before he met me. I thought that was pretty interesting too."

"I'll say. But that still doesn't really explain why you're alone now. Didn't you mention some guy...Sam?"

She took the last bite of her stew and was silent for a bit, wondering how far she should go with this.

"After the divorce, I went to a kind of spiritual conference where the leader helped me see that really I wasn't ready for commitment in the way I'd thought, that I also didn't want to give myself fully to a deep relationship. And that at some level, I'd intentionally chosen a partner who would make it impossible to have a real marriage. All that was unconscious of course at the time, but it's left me a bit wary. Let's just say I've gotten used to being alone. And honestly, I don't ever want to be in a position to go through what I went through with Jason ever again. Guess I'm just afraid to get serious about someone. I have friends, some with benefits, as they say. And Sam is a great business partner, which can be almost like a marriage. It's not like I'm a recluse."

Something in her tone suggested there was more to this thing with Sam.

"But don't you miss it? Being in love?" Matt's romantic nature was kindled.

"I try not to think about it. Have to admit though, I do get teary-eyed when I see a movie with a good love story." She smiled wistfully.

"Okay, this will sound weird, since I'm a guy saying this to a girl. You seem like a nice woman who deserves to have a good man in her life. Makes me kind of sad that you don't."

"Thanks…" She squirmed a bit, and Matt could see he'd pushed her further than she'd wanted to go on that subject. Finally, she said, "So what about you?"

He dropped his head and got real quiet. After a minute, he looked up and said, "I was married for a while to Amanda, love of my life. But after I got back from Iraq, things fell apart and…"

his voice trailed, "she left me."

"Oh, Matt, I'm so sorry. I can see that hurt you a lot." She began to feel the source of the pain she'd sensed in him earlier.

"Yeah," he answered dejectedly. "Maybe we both need to talk about something else."

She knew the energy that had propelled them down this path of closeness was dissipating rapidly. He clearly needed space now.

"Agreed," she said lightly. "Want to help me clean up?"

"Sure. That sounds like a great idea." He stood up quickly.

They brought everything back inside, and she washed the dishes while he carried food to the truck. At one point, she glanced at the clock and was surprised to see it was almost nine. They'd been talking for quite a while. *Yeah, well, he's easy to talk to, and damn easy on the eyes too.*

When Matt came back in, he said, "You know, it's getting late. I think I'm going to turn in."

The tone in his voice was almost apologetic. Still, there was a finality to the pronouncement. He had pulled away.

"Me too. It has been a really nice evening, Matt."

She reached out to hug him. All her friends were huggers, and it was almost a reflexive act now, but she felt him stiffen when she wrapped her arms around him. *Oops, guess he's not into that. Massive bummer cause he feels good.*

"It has, Nicole. Thanks for dinner, and the drinks. Maybe I'll see you tomorrow."

"That would be great. Have a good night." She felt the pull of not wanting him to leave.

"Yeah, good night," he said, and the hint of reluctance in his voice was palpable.

Still, he left.

chapter
3

As he neared his own camping space, Matt shook his head, perplexed. He had not come up here to get involved with a woman, and yet he felt himself captivated by *this* woman, Nicole. He couldn't put his finger on it—what exactly it was about her that made him feel so… *safe*. Boy that was a word he hadn't used in a long time. But there it was, he felt safe talking to her, like he could trust her, this stranger. Jeez, he'd only known her for a few hours, and honestly he hadn't said all that much. But her openness, her air of easy acceptance, drew him into a peace he had not experienced before. He shook his head again.

Pulling a chair close to the campsite table, he sat for a while looking up at the stars. Wow, a million of them. *Don't see that in the city*. The moon wasn't up yet, so nothing blocked their light. He found as many constellations as he could remember before he got too sleepy to think anymore. Then he crawled into his tent, stripped down and zipped up his sleeping bag. His last thoughts as he drifted off were of Nicole dancing.

Nicole zipped up the windows of the camper and closed the curtains. Then she flopped down on the bench and puzzled over everything that had happened that evening. She could feel how they'd been starting to click. But then why did Matt flinch when she had tried to hug him? Even if he didn't do that as a norm with his friends, the reaction had seemed to be more than just discomfort with something unfamiliar.

And he hadn't opened up much about himself. In fact, he'd hardly said anything. *Maybe he's a serial killer up here to find his next victim,* that off-the-wall voice inside her said. But no, she'd felt his energy, could see in his eyes that he was, deep down, a pretty gentle soul. Definitely strong, sensual, tight body, and very much a man. Troubled, that was it. *That guy's got a story to tell.*

How had he gotten her to go on about her own story? She hadn't said that much about her relationship with Jason to anyone for years, not even to her sister, Jen. Not exactly her favorite thing to think about, though she had tried hard for a while to understand it all.

The conference she'd gone to, in a retreat center in the desert of Arizona, was the first step she'd taken toward that end. The meditation calmed her, and the energy of the group of souls in search of deeper truth had opened her up to seeing a broader view. Her work with the spiritual teacher, in circle, had offered some clarity about the relationship. What she'd just told Matt—that she wasn't ready for commitment—was quite a simplification. Going into that last fight with Jason before she left, she'd earnestly believed she wanted the marriage and that it was Jason's perceived insincerity that had her feeling like she needed to get out. But when Jason had asked her point blank what was the real reason for leaving, she'd found herself suddenly blurting out that she just hadn't played the field enough yet, she wasn't ready to settle down. Even now, Nicole couldn't believe she'd said that. The words had sounded foreign the moment they came out of her mouth. It was her teacher who, after listening patiently to her tale, quietly and with great compassion said, "Yes, and also."

"It's true you felt insecure in a relationship that did not seem to mean as much to your husband as it did to you," he had told her. "Clearly the part of you that you identify with, the one you usually know yourself as, believes that *yes*, you want the commitment of marriage. Yet your remark to your husband suggests there is another part of you, which you have now caught a glimpse of. This part of you wants something entirely different. She's wanting to be free, might even be afraid of commitment.

"Which becomes the *and also*. That part of you didn't want to be in such a close relationship. In fact, that part of you might very well have not spoken to Jason about his flirting and so on, because she wanted that excuse to leave. Most people in your situation would have talked to their partner about the behavior that was causing concern. You did not.

"So what we have here is two parts of your being that are at odds with one another. It will be up to you to work with them, perhaps find a resolution. Or not. To be discovered."

Yes, she felt insecure in a relationship that did not seem to mean as much to her husband as it did to her; she believed she wanted the commitment of marriage. *And also*, she herself didn't want to be in such a close relationship; she wanted to be free.

As he spoke, she began to feel these contradictory parts of her being, caught in a dance that could only end in the demise of her marriage. She felt the truth that she had, at a deep, unfathomable level, intentionally chosen a man who would give her reason to get out. She'd left the conference in awe of the intricate enigma she and Jason had been. Yet she still didn't understand the part of her that would rather be free than be genuinely attached, especially to someone like Sam who loved her so completely.

Inwardly she sighed and turned her thoughts to this new man who had abruptly entered her life. They were drawn to each other, undoubtedly, and yet he'd also kept his distance, as though he just couldn't let himself go there.

Yeah, this man, Matt, is a real mystery, she thought as she got ready for bed and turned out the lights. *Wonder if I'll see him tomorrow.*

chapter 4

Nicole woke to the sound of birds singing and the feel of sunlight streaming in across her face. *Another beautiful day in paradise.* She threw on clothes and gathered quarters, shampoo and towel for the shower. The private campground had showers—such a luxury. There was no way she could go a week without a real shower.

Matt's Jeep was in his site, but he was nowhere to be seen when she left the camper for the walk to the shower building. Must've been sleeping in. As she made her way down the hill, she thought again about the evening before. Well, more about the man than the evening. God, he was intriguing. She'd loved just looking at his face, watching him move. Honestly, she hadn't been this attracted to anyone in a very long time. And admittedly, it was more than just physical. There was also a deep connection on, what? A soulic level? She'd stopped believing in coincidence years ago, so what must this mean? If it wasn't an accident that they'd been put next to each other, here, now, then what was in store for them?

It was early enough that no one else was in the shower building when she arrived. She loved having the space all to herself so she could take her time. Nicole put her bag on the bench, took the shampoo and quarters to the slot machine, and stripped down. One quarter gave her three minutes to get wet all over and clean most of her body. When the water stopped, she got the shampoo and washed her hair. Another quarter gave her another three minutes to rinse it out and just enjoy the warmth of the water running over her, as well as time to fantasize what it would be like to have Matt's hands running over her body. *Oh, wow*. The water stopped. *Cut it out, honey. There were no signs last night that he was interested in you in that way. Give it a rest.*

She dried off and got dressed as quickly as she could. It was chilly. It would warm up later, though. With any luck, there would be a small thunderstorm this afternoon. Thunderstorms were her favorite weather, and it was especially delightful when she could lie in the camper and hear the raindrops plopping down on the canvas over her bed. It was the best way in the world to take a nap.

Nicole drank in the sunshine as she walked back to the camper. When she came around the corner near her campsite, she saw that Matt's Jeep was gone. The sudden stab of disappointment surprised her. This guy had really gotten under her skin. *Ah well.*

She dried her hair, gathered up her iPad, purse and keys. The diner just up the road had Wi-Fi, and she loved going there for breakfast and to check email, not to mention the views of the mountain river on the drive up there. She smiled inside as she drove her truck out of the campground.

The diner was not exactly busy this morning. There were just two older couples at tables across the room from each other. The hostess motioned her to sit where she liked, and Nicole chose the booth she'd sat in many times in summers past. The place was homey, furnished in mountain-style tables and chairs, and had dark red leather booths along one side. There was lots of wood everywhere—log walls, beamed ceilings, rough-hewn counters. A huge stone fireplace in the corner topped it all off.

When she was settled and had had time to look over the menu, the waitress came back to take her order.

"Good morning. Want some coffee to get started?"

"Yes, please. With cream," Nicole said with a smile.

"You got it. Be right back."

Nicole already knew what she wanted for breakfast. With the smell of bacon in the air, was there any doubt? It was time to check email.

As expected, there was one from Sam. Sam, such a central part of her life, as a dear friend and business partner. Sam, who loved her deeply, even though she did not have the same kind of love to return. Oh, she loved him—who wouldn't? He was so funny and kind, adorable, but as a friend now. She couldn't allow herself to go beyond that.

If she was really honest with herself, she had loved him too, from the first moment they met. Something had made her look up just as he'd walked in the door at the Cheyenne Frontier Days staff meeting, and their eyes locked. His sensuous mouth had widened in a slow, lazy smile that perfectly matched the way he moved, with the ease and grace of a man who knew his body well, and how to use it. She'd fallen right then, hard, and as they began working together on plans for the event, it was obvious they'd really clicked.

Sam was so funny. He could always make her laugh (especially at the most inopportune times!), yet he'd also been quite vulnerable with her. On the anniversary of his father's death, Sam had told her how much he'd regretted not spending more time with him, told her some of the hurtful things he'd said to his father the day he left home. Sam had broken down in tears, and Nicole held him tenderly, let him cry it out. The connection forged that day would last forever.

She flashed on the feelings that had welled up in her when he'd taken her to see one of his kung fu matches. Watching his muscular, graceful body overpowering his opponent had excited her more than she could admit. After the last round, he'd come over to her and helped her down the bleacher stairs. His arms were so strong to lean on and his hands so gentle on her waist. But at the time, he had not made a move on her, and they were, after all, coworkers who "shouldn't" get involved. Barely a year past the divorce from Jason, she didn't want to be in a relationship anyway. She'd held down her desires.

So it had all been just hanging out together, all casual-like, until that particularly grueling after-event meeting. They were the last to leave, and as they were walking down the long hall, Sam suddenly pressed Nicole firmly to the wall with his whole body, hands gently holding her face, and kissed her, hard. She'd responded at first, flamed at his compelling touch. Then something inside her panicked, and she'd pushed him away. He'd mumbled an apology, and she—unable to grasp why she'd rejected him—was too embarrassed to try to explain. He'd quickly made a joke to break the tension, and they'd both pretended it hadn't happened.

After some months though, he'd finally gotten the courage to tell her how he felt.

Sam had given her a lift home after a night out with friends. When they arrived at her house, he'd quickly hopped out of the car and come around to open her door—an uncharacteristic move for him. She'd made it clear early on she wasn't into that. And he was distinctly nervous as he walked her to the porch. Puzzled, she stood waiting for him to speak.

"Nicole," he sputtered, and then hurriedly poured out his heart. "You have to know I love you. You're the sweetest, most fun woman I've ever known. And it's wonderful being friends with you, but I really want more. I want us to be together. I want us to share our lives."

He'd paused then, afraid to hear her response. When she said nothing, but looked at him with wide eyes, he'd awkwardly grabbed her and pulled her close to kiss her. But he'd misjudged, pulled too hard, and they both tumbled to the floor in a heap. Nicole had burst out laughing, then feeling his body on hers, feeling the love he'd expressed, kissed him tenderly.

So they'd had a shot at being a true couple. She'd been unsure, torn between the love she'd known she had for Sam and the still gnawing fear. Sam had been on cloud nine, but she couldn't hold it. It had broken his heart when she ended it.

How could she ever forget that awful day? She'd just dropped him off at his place after having dinner with friends. He'd invited her in, as usual, but as she went through the front door, the strain inside her peaked. The door closed behind her, and she broke.

"Sam." She had been so afraid to say the words. The words she knew could destroy everything they'd built together. "Sam, I can't do this anymore. I know you really love me, and I love you too. I do. But I can't be this close, be your…girlfriend. I don't even know how to explain it to you. It's freaking me out."

"Nicole, I don't understand. We're good together." The pain on his face tore at her heart.

"Sam, I wish I could say something that would make sense, but I don't understand it either. I just know that there's a tension in me that just keeps building, and building, and it's becoming like this panic. This awful feeling that *I have to get free*. Jeez, Sam..." She dropped her head in her hands and sobbed.

Sam was stunned. They'd been so happy, for months now. Though he hadn't yet brought up the subject of marriage, he'd been looking at rings, wanting to share the rest of his life with her.

"Nicole." He reached out and lifted her chin. "Please. Tell me what I can do. I can't lose you..." He broke down then, crying.

"Sam, I don't want to lose you either. Your friendship means more to me than I can say. I just can't be a couple anymore." Again, she dropped her head and in a small voice begged, "Forgive me."

"Oh my God, Nicole, please don't tell me this is over forever. Please tell me you're just needing a break, that you'll come back to me. That we can be friends only for now, but someday we'll be more again."

"Maybe. I don't know. Sam, I can't promise more than that now. Maybe..."

She'd probably never forgive herself for what she'd done next. Jumping right into seeing someone else. That had really strained their friendship. For a while, it wasn't at all certain they could even continue the business together. It helped some when Sam also started up with another woman. But of course that hadn't lasted long. He'd broken it off within a few weeks. His heart belonged to Nicole.

And so they'd settled into what they had now. They were friends, while he waited for her to want to be more again. He was her teddy bear, her confidant—even about her infrequent and short-lived relationships with other guys—and her rock. He was the one she could always count on. She couldn't imagine her life without him.

Heavily she sighed, and then read his email.

Hey, 'sup? How's the camping hermit?

Great. You know how being up here feeds my soul. How are things on your end?

She didn't expect an immediate answer, but apparently Sam was online so they chatted.

Getting interesting. I've got a possible in with Hayley Ross through her agent, Ginger. You know Hayley's engaged to Mark Harrison, don't you? Apparently, they want to do a small wedding right here in Cheyenne. I talked to Ginger a while, and they all want to meet. I don't have the final yes since they need to talk to you first, but it sure looks likely we'll get the job.

Wonderful! I'll have something to do when I get back.

Yes, you will. Both work and play. I've got some friends from college coming out in a couple weeks, and they want to try rafting. I've already talked to Jen and Nick, so they're up for it too. Means you have to tag along.

That actually sounds like fun. I haven't been rafting in what, four years? Remember when we went with that group from Frontier Days?

Oh God, that was a blast. I'd forgotten about that. So we're on?

Yep.

Fantastic. See you in a few.

The waitress came back with coffee, Nicole's wake-up juice of choice, and to get her order. A little cream, a little sugar, and a big sip, and Nicole was ready to tackle email again.

Ah, here's one from Jen.

Hey sis. Sam just called and wants to go rafting in a few weeks. He has some friends coming. We've got a babysitter lined up, and we're going. Can you come too?

Yeah, just read Sam's email about it. I'm in.

She concentrated on getting more coffee into her system while she waited for her food to arrive. Up popped a response from Jen.

Bet Sam looks really good in swim trunks. You should be watching...

Yeah, yeah.

She decided not to tell Jen about Matt yet. After all, what was there to tell? That she had the hots for some random guy who was camping next to her? One she probably wouldn't have more than casual conversations with? Well, maybe not just casual—how *had* he gotten her to say so much about Jason? The guy was definitely more than just eye-candy.

Breakfast came, so she flipped to a book she'd been reading. After a chapter, she went back to her email. Why was this author so popular, considering she had so much repetition in her style? There were a few more emails she needed to respond to, but they could wait until later—this was a vacation after all.

chapter 5

Matt had woken with a jolt when his alarm went off. He'd wanted to get an early start on his trip to Carson Lake. He dressed hurriedly, grabbed his fishing gear, several bottles of water and a couple protein bars, and drove his Jeep very slowly and quietly out of the campground. As he passed Nicole's camper, he thought again of the woman who had so drawn him in, inexplicably. How had their conversation made him feel like she could see him, really see him? How had that made him feel that strong desire to be physically *with* her? He hadn't even let himself feel that for Amanda. He shook his head. He didn't want to think about Nicole right now. *Fishing only.*

Certainly, he loved the beaches and ocean waves of his hometown—he was a Cali surfer dude after all—but this drive to the lake was somehow even more serene. *Could be the lack of people,* he thought. San Diego was so crowded. No matter how early you got there, you were never alone on the beach. There was a lot to be said for just being alone, with yourself, with all this rugged beauty around you. It made him feel solidly connected to life, like he belonged here, just as he was. Maybe that was what people meant when they said they felt centered.

His was the first car to park at the trailhead, another novelty. The fishing gear and small cooler weren't heavy, and he started out easily on the clearly marked trail. It was well maintained, much better than the ones in the hills near his home. Again, there were too many people there, and they left so much trash. He wondered if maybe Wyoming people had a better appreciation of the land.

The trail climbed pretty steeply for a while. When he got to the high point, he found a log to sit on while he took in the view of the lake below him and guzzled down one of his bottles of water. Between the altitude and the drier air of the mountains, he felt thirsty. His breathing gradually settled from the exertion of the hike so far. The altitude had affected him this way too. Back home, the climbing would have been quite easy, as exercise was a daily habit for him. The Army had started that; basic training was intense. Now he liked how he felt when he pushed his body to be stronger and liked how he looked. Being purely physical also gave him a break from the anguish he felt about Iraq, about Amanda…

Eventually, Matt's gaze turned from one that took in the whole scene before him to picking out possible fishing spots. Just a short distance down from him looked like a good one, so he picked up his gear and started out again. He passed a fellow fisherman who told him the place he'd picked would likely yield as many fish as he was allowed. And if not, there was one over there—he pointed—that would do well too.

Setting up his fishing spot, tying on his fly—an elk hair caddis he'd had since he was a kid—and then casting out brought back many memories of fishing with his dad. Man, those had been great times. Just the two of them camping for several days and eating their catch every night. Matt laughed out loud, remembering the first fish he'd caught. He was only seven, and the little trout had only been about nine inches long. Normally, they would throw trout that small back in, but he was a kid determined to eat what he'd caught. So his dad fried it up that night. It was still the best fish he'd ever eaten.

He really missed those times with his dad. They weren't close anymore. The death of his mom while Matt was in high school, killed when a drunk driver smashed into her, had started his dad's withdrawal. She was his first love, and he was lost without her. It had taken ten years for his dad to move past the tragedy. He was happily remarried now. But the distance between him and his sons hadn't completely healed. All three had just grown apart. It got worse when Matt had decided to join the Army. His dad could not understand Matt leaving his new bride, Amanda, for so long, especially since he was still grieving and missing his own wife. Then Matt returned from Iraq, wouldn't talk about it, and his dad felt shut out. Not long after, the split with Amanda came, and still Matt would not explain what was really going on with him. Finally, they stopped talking, except for the obligatory holidays. It saddened Matt horribly, but he just couldn't tell his dad about what had happened that horrible night in Iraq, what he'd seen, what he'd done, what he hadn't done…

And Amanda. His wife. He could see her face clearly as she stood on the altar, smiling at him, her eyes filled with love and tears. He remembered how it felt to touch her face, kiss her mouth, hold her close. The long nights of sharing the secrets of their souls, making love until dawn. Thoughts of their squabbles brought a smile to his lips because they'd never lasted long. The love always overcame the disagreements. They'd planned so carefully for the future, wanted the same things out of life, even playfully talked about baby names. She filled his life with so much bliss. Until Iraq.

Memories of their last big blowup before she left came rushing back.

Amanda had pleaded, demanded, "Matt, you have to tell me what's going on with you. Otherwise, what do we have? A relationship is nothing without communication."

His voice tight with pain, he could only say, "I can't, Amanda. I just can't."

They looked at each other mournfully as the chasm widened between them. He dropped his eyes.

"Then *I* can't. I can't do this anymore, Matt." Angrily, she'd turned on her heel and walked out.

He really didn't want to believe it was over, but it was. God, he missed her...

Okay dude, you're up here to enjoy the fishing. Stop thinking about all this stuff.

He forced his mind back to the scenery. And the sun on his face. And the forever blue sky above. And his line in the water. Slowly, Matt relaxed back into the day.

chapter 6

The view of the river from the bridge leading to the campground was one of her favorites. All that fresh mountain water tumbling over the rocks. It could actually be quite dangerous as fast moving as it was, especially in the spring when all the winter snowpack started to melt, and people who weren't careful did get swept away, some never to be seen again in this life. And yet there was something exciting about the river's headlong rush to the sea.

Nicole decided to walk down to the little beach and hang out when she got back.

Now that the sun was fully up, it was getting pretty warm. Altitude does that; when the air's thin, sun versus no sun makes all the difference in the temperature. It was time for shorts and sandals. She gathered her journal, water, iPod and earplugs and headed down to the river.

When she passed Matt's campsite, she was again reminded of what he'd told her last night, that she deserved to have a good man in her life. He was so sweet to say that. *Maybe that was an offer? Hmm, no, I don't think so.* She had to admit to herself that she'd kind of been feeling that way too as of late. It really was about time, the clock ticking and all. She didn't want to be single forever.

She made her way down to the little sandy strip by the river and found a flat rock to sit on. Her eyes drank in the scene—cold clear water, jagged rock walls of the canyon, infinite blue sky, and random colorful wildflowers strewn amongst the pine trees—all perfectly combined to make the magical rocky mountain picture. Taking a few deep, cleansing breaths, she put in her earbuds and selected a meditation piece that always helped her get centered. When she could feel that calmness, she began her inner work.

Thinking about all she'd told Matt the evening before, about Jason, took her back to the time just after they'd split. The experience of being with a man who professed to love her but was so attentive to others had left her confused, disoriented. Her faith in whatever this "love" thing was supposed to be had been badly shaken. A friend at the time hinted that her spiritual teacher might have some insights for her, so she'd signed up for one of his conferences—his basic course. It had changed her life in a profound way. He'd opened her eyes to archetypes, oracles, new perspectives, a much broader way of looking at life. Still, even though they'd worked with a dream she'd had about Jason during the conference, and she'd grasped the "yes and also" about why she'd left, she'd had no breakthrough in the underlying dynamic that kept her from being in a committed relationship.

Again, she went through it all in her mind—the same "reasons" whirling around like they always did. Was she afraid of being abandoned? Just afraid of being hurt again? She tried over and over to get down to the bottom of her fears, but nothing felt like it was really the *answer*. Especially when she put Sam in the mix. The man loved her with all his heart. He wouldn't abandon her, wouldn't hurt her, had been patiently waiting for her for years. While he rarely spoke it aloud these days, he made it clear to her in so many ways. When they'd been more than friends, that brief three months of a full-on relationship, she'd mostly felt secure and loved. And *in* love. They were so close, so in sync. He'd opened himself completely, sharing the deepest parts of himself, and she did too. Except for that one small piece of her that got more and more panicky, pushing her to leave. *What the hell? It makes no sense. I should be able to figure this out.* Finally, in frustration, she walked back up to the camper.

What in the world was *really* holding her back?

By early afternoon Matt had given up on catching fish. Either that fisherman he'd talked to had been really off the mark in his advice, or had intentionally led him astray. Though he also had to admit it had been a half-hearted attempt on his part. Really, he was just up here to chill, after all. Mission accomplished. He decided to head back, maybe see what Nicole was up to.

Nicole. His mind was immediately filled with the image of her light brown hair falling to her shoulders, those soft blue eyes, and warm smile that lit him up inside. Her graceful body that so loved to dance. *Man, I'd like to dance with her, and clothes are optional.* The thought both thrilled him and depressed him. *You know why you can't be thinking like that.*

Still, as he drove into the campground, to the upper loop and his campsite, the only thing on his mind, for a change, was Nicole.

chapter 7

Nicole looked up from the iPad and sighed. *Done with that book,* she thought. *Not really all that great, but at least now I can say I've read it.* She gazed lovingly at the pine trees and the steep rocky mountain on the other side of the boulder-strewn river. She breathed in deeply. *God, I love being up here, alone.*

As she walked back into the camper to put the iPad away, she thought again of the gorgeous man—*Matt*—who was camping next to her and now seemed like he could be in her life somehow. *How did that even happen?* she wondered. She guessed it would still be a while before he got back from wherever he'd been. She had time for a drink and some tunes.

She'd recently spent some time making a great playlist of her favorite dance music. While she'd always been more of a rock fan—both classics and now alternative rock—a couple years ago she'd started to like the newer country as well. There were a few songs on her list that were faster, but the ones she really liked were the slow, slinky rhythms that reached deep into her pelvis for expression. And so she started with "Fast Cars and Freedom" by Rascal Flatts, moving her hips in the circles and figure eights she'd learned years ago in a belly dancing class. She could feel that part of herself so confident in her sexuality coming up. She hadn't been strongly in touch with that for a while now. Lost in the sensual world of music and movement, she barely heard the knock on the door.

She whirled around, and there was Matt all blue jeans and gray T-shirt and tousled hair and those searching blue eyes. He reached for her hand, to dance with her, and she was thrilled at the sight of his hips moving in time with hers. *Oh my, he can dance!*

"How was your morning?" She tried to sound casual to cover the desire building in her.

"So great. Went to Carson Lake, hiked around, found a good fishing spot. Didn't catch anything, which is okay cause I hate to clean fish. I can't believe I never bothered to come to Wyoming sooner. I'm totally hooked now. How was your day?"

"Finally finished this book I've been reading. Kind of a disappointment."

The song ended, and Ray Scott began singing "Gypsy" in that deep sexy voice he has. In sync with the slow sensual rhythm, Matt pulled her closer, one hand lightly on her waist and one hand holding hers. There was still a small space between their bodies, but she could feel his heat, smell his earthy smell. As they swayed back and forth, all thought of talking disappeared completely. His focus was all on those sensuous hips rocking in time to the music, completely in unison with his own. *What would they feel like, underneath me?* He pulled even closer, his cheek touching hers, and put her hand on his chest just as Ray hummed the closing *Mmmmm* of the song.

There was no mistaking his intentions now. She felt the warmth of his skin under the shirt, felt his heartbeat. *Mmmm indeed. This man is sexy as hell.* Both his hands were on her waist now, and her arm went about his neck as she melted into him. Her breasts pressed against his muscled chest. *Oh, I'm so glad I took that awful bra off earlier.* His head left hers for a moment, and she felt his soft kiss on her neck, burning through the most exquisite parts of her. They swayed languidly to the music, lost in the exotic feelings of body on body.

Now Jake Owens was singing "Alone with You" and they moved to the new rhythm, the building anticipation consuming them both. Matt's hand had slipped further down her back so he could pull her hips even closer, and as Jake sang about slipping hands under shirts, she did just that, running her hand up his chest, feeling his tight abs, the soft hair over his nipple. She heard him suck in his breath at her touch. Suddenly his arms left her, and with one swift movement, he had pulled his shirt off over his head.

He looked questioningly into her eyes, *will this be okay?* While her eyes answered *yes*, she ran her fingertips down his chest to his stomach and along the top of his jeans. He took her face in his hands and kissed her long and slow, then pulled her shirt off too. Skin to skin they danced, hands roaming, searching each other, and as Jake sang about falling, they both knew it had already happened for them. He kissed her passionately on the mouth, and she felt to the tips of her toes how strong and sensual his lips were. Deep down she felt the fire, and the longing. He cupped her breasts in his hands while she ran her thumbs over his nipples, and they moaned together. Their kisses got stronger and needier until finally the music faded from their awareness altogether, and they moved to the edge of the bed.

Suddenly, he stopped and pulled back. There was an unmistakable look of anguish on his face that she couldn't understand—weren't they doing fine until now? She looked into his eyes, and her heart reached out to his, saying, "It's okay, please, Matt." She stroked his cheek and gave him a soft kiss. The fear slowly drained from his eyes as a consuming desire took its place.

Gently, she pushed him onto the bed, and they began the intimate dance all lovers do, with soft searching touch that moves into the pressing and grinding of two bodies demanding to become one.

The feeling of him filling her was heaven itself, but then he began to move his hips in slow circles, and heaven expanded to fireworks of colors and intensities she'd never experienced before. His own cry of ecstasy made her joy complete.

Tenderly, they kissed and held each other close. *Ooh, my God.*

chapter 8

They lay together for a long time, holding each other, she gently stroking his arm and his chest. She could tell he was struggling with something. He was trembling. He wouldn't speak though, so she just held him to her heart. When she kissed him softly on the cheek, he looked up, and she saw tears in his eyes.

"Oh, Matt. You're very precious," she whispered.

The look in his eyes turned to shock, and she could feel his energy withdraw as he suddenly pulled away. *What?*

He was in turmoil. *She can't mean that. She doesn't know*. He could not let her words in, refused. He gathered himself as best he could and said, "I'm really hungry. Is there someplace around here we could get something to eat?"

The radical shift in him was inexplicable to her. Clearly, something was off, but she had no idea what it could be. *We were incredible together. What could be so wrong now?* But she followed his lead and said, "Yeah, there's a retro diner not far from here. Want to try that?"

"Sounds good," he said tersely.

They dressed in silence—he in shame and uncertainty; she in confusion and concern for him.

And they didn't talk much on the way to the restaurant. They were in his Jeep, so she gave him directions, and periodically she would point out a special view or amazing rock formation. It seemed to calm him down a bit, seeing the beauty in the world. When they arrived and got out of the Jeep, she walked over to him and gave him a friendly, heartfelt hug. At first, he couldn't accept it, tensed up, but when she made it clear she wasn't going away, he let it in and tentatively hugged her back.

The restaurant was one of her favorites. The owner was a guy who'd wanted to drop out, so to speak, and live the laid-back life he had in college. Done in sixties decor, there were posters of Hendrix and Morrison and Beatles and others, all with black lights. The booths were plush and the floors cork. You felt kind of high just walking into the place. And of course, the best sixties rock and roll music was coming from speakers all around the room. Not too loud, just loud enough that it helped drown out conversations from others in the room. The hostess, wearing bell-bottom jeans, a Rolling Stones T-shirt and a fringed leather vest, sat them at a booth in the corner and handed them menus.

"Hi, I'm Janice, and I'll be taking care of you tonight. Want something to drink?"

Matt ordered a margarita and Nicole a lemon drop martini.

"Great. I'll be right back with those," Janice said and danced away to the music.

They quickly looked at the menus and decided what to order. Both of them needed to talk. Nicole started.

"What happened, Matt? What's wrong?"

"It's definitely not you, Nicole," he said, looking sheepishly into her eyes. "You're great."

"Then what is it? What made you pull away?"

"It has to do with my time in the Army. That was a rough time." He dropped his eyes to gather himself again.

"Do you want to tell me about it?"

He looked up at her. *She'd be so easy to talk to. Maybe...*

Janice came back then with their drinks.

"What are you all having tonight? The trout is fresh, just caught today, if you're interested in that."

"Oh, trout sounds great. I'll have that," Nicole said.

"Burger for me, with cheese, and fries," said Matt.

"I'll get that right away."

After she left, Matt hesitated, unsure just how far he could let himself go with this. "I guess so. But I have to start further back. I'm a surfer kid from San Diego. Did I tell you that? Never really had any idea what I would do after college. So I went for three years and dropped out. I was just so lost, felt clueless about myself, what my life should be. I had an uncle who'd made a career of the Army, and when he suggested it might be good for me, I jumped on it. I mean, what the hell. I didn't know what else to do."

"Sometimes it helps to have the discipline, the narrow rules, to figure out who you are."

"Yeah, that's exactly it. Basic training was tough, no doubt about that. But I started to find my strengths, know my limits. I gained some confidence in myself, felt like I could contribute to something beyond conquering a wave, getting a good grade on a test. Then I got shipped off to Iraq."

His face went dark then, and he had to take deep breaths before he could go on. "At first, I was in an area that wasn't seeing much action. We just did patrols and such, to make our presence known and watch for any signs of trouble. The guys I was with, we got to be good friends..."

His eyes got so sad she thought he might cry. She wondered if maybe some of them hadn't made it back.

Janice came to the table then with their food. Nicole tried to make small talk with her, to keep Matt from having to say anything. The waitress was astute, could see something was going on between her customers, and left them alone after she was sure they had what they needed.

"Matt, are you okay?"

"Yeah...not really. Let's just say it got worse after we were moved north to a town where radicals had taken hold." He looked dejectedly at his food.

Clearly, neither of them was going to be able to eat with this topic on the table, so Nicole shifted the direction.

"You know, I have to admit I really know very little about Iraq, what the country's like, what the people are like."

He brightened a bit. "Parts of the country are beautiful, rolling hills, rivers and fertile fields. Even the desert areas are peaceful in their own way. And the history of the area is beyond compare. I mean, you know—the cradle of civilization. But it's the people who are really amazing. They've been through so much, especially recently, and yet they are gracious and hard working. You can see in everything they do the gratitude they feel. They view life as a gift not to be taken for granted. So different from what you see here in the States where so many people think they should just be handed everything."

"Do you think that's because of their faith?"

"Some. Even the Iraqis I met who didn't seem all that strongly religious would be on their knees every day with the ones who were. Felt like there was something about that act that kept them humble, connected to something more than just everyday life."

"Oh, I can see that. Everyone needs a reminder every now and then that life isn't actually centered around them."

"Exactly. Watching them, getting to know them a little, made me want to understand them better. Not the Quran as such. I wanted to know where they came from, their culture. It's not like we had much time to read, but when I could get my hands on some books, I read about the history of that area. It really clicked with me." He was almost glowing now, clearly passionate about this subject. And he was certainly enjoying his food.

Nicole kept him talking about Iraq's history, its culture and its people. The conversation expanded to other countries and cultures as well, and Nicole loved hearing him talk about it all. He had read so much, was so knowledgeable and seemed to have a broad understanding of how the different cultures had shaped their history.

Abruptly, he said, "So now, enough of that. Tell me about Sam."

Nicole took in a deep breath. "I met him not long after my divorce, after that conference I told you about. We definitely hit it off—he's so wonderful. But I wasn't really ready to be in a relationship yet. Not after Jason."

"I can imagine. Anyone would be gun-shy after that experience."

"Still, I let Sam talk me into the boyfriend/girlfriend thing. We did that for several months, and Sam was great. I just couldn't do it so soon…I ended it. Badly. Very badly. We went back to being just good friends, but he really wants more, and I let him think it might happen again. So basically, he's waiting for me."

"Wow, that's rough. Didn't you say you have friends with benefits? How does he manage that?"

"Well, we've both had other people in our lives, not just me. And yeah, it hurts him a lot. Honestly, I don't know why he's still in love with me, but he is." She sighed heavily.

"Sorry, Nicole. Didn't mean to bring up stuff that would make you uncomfortable. It was just something in your tone when you talked about him before that made me wonder if maybe you had strong feelings for him."

"I do. But I don't know what to do with them, so I guess I've kind of pushed them to the background, if you know what I mean."

He could see she was tapped out about the topic of Sam, so he asked her questions about her childhood. And they were off again, sharing funny stories about themselves as kids. By the time they were done with their meal, both of them were grinning and chatting happily.

chapter 9

They continued talking on the way back to the campground, about his growing up in San Diego, her growing up in Cheyenne. They spoke about music, movies and books. And by the time they pulled up to her camper, they were both ready for another drink.

"How about I fix us a couple of margis, and you put on some tunes?" Matt asked.

Nicole turned on the miniature Coleman lantern string lights, giving the camper's interior a soft glow.

"Sounds wonderful. Listening music or dance music?"

Dance. The word instantly brought up visions of the last time, and his head brain shut off, the lower one taking full control.

"Ummm, dance," he said and moved his body in the most delicious way. She melted.

"Oh-kay," was all she could get out.

Matt fixed the margis while she found her dance mix and

started it. As the first strains moved to her hips, she swayed over to Matt, took the drink he offered, and they began a slow sensuous dance. Eyes locked on each other's bodies, they mirrored each other's moves, still not touching, but so in unison, it was just as intimate, just as intense. Looking deeply into Matt's eyes, Nicole could feel the essence of this strong, tender man.

Suddenly he said, "Now chug," and they both finished their drinks and put down the glasses. With hands free, the dancing turned to seductive exploring. When they kissed, his lips were demanding and firm, and she echoed the desire that was building inside him.

"Nicole, I need you so bad," he panted. He lifted her onto the bed, and with an intensity and urgency both knew came from the very depths of his being, made love to her.

As they lay side by side in the sleeping bag, Matt marveled at this extraordinary woman beside him. She had opened him up in a way he hadn't thought possible, brought him back to a part of himself he'd feared was forever lost. He gently stroked her arm as they drifted off into sleep.

He woke violently, thrashing about, terrified. Just as she awoke, he cried out, and she could hear the utter anguish in it. She reached over to turn on the lantern beside the bed, took him in her arms and held him close to her heart. He trembled and broke, sobbing into her breasts like a child. She caressed his back and spoke his name softly until it passed.

"Nicole, I'm so sorry," he finally mumbled.

"Jesus, Matt, don't be sorry. What happened?" She lifted his chin, so he could see her eyes.

"I had another one of these horrible dreams I have."

"Do you want to tell me about it?"

He hid his face again, unable to let her see who and what he was. So ashamed, he couldn't burden her with his madness.

"No, seriously, you don't want to hear it. It's completely awful." He began to tremble again, and her heart went out to him. She stroked his hair, tenderly.

"Yes, Matt, I do. You're obviously in so much pain. Let me share it."

"You're really sweet to say that, but you don't know." His breath hitched, and he looked like he was about to fall to pieces. "You'll hate me if you know what's inside me."

She looked him square in the eye, into his soul, and said, "I really think I can handle it, Matt. Please tell me."

His heart pounded in his tense body, still in a panic from the intensity of the dream, so it took him a while to gather himself enough to consider it. Then he took a deep, shaky breath and looked at her. *How could I say such things to this woman? I barely know her*. But she held his gaze, steadily, and he consented.

"Can we get up, have a drink? I'll need it to calm me if I'm going to get this out. And I have a feeling you'll need it too, after you hear the nightmare my life is."

"Of course," she said. She held his face in her hands and kissed him gently on the forehead before she got up.

It was cold in the camper, so she turned up the heat, and they both got blankets to wrap up in. She poured two glasses of wine, and they sat down at the table. He took a long drink, looked at her mournfully and with a heavy sigh began.

"I've told you I was stationed in Iraq. And that some very unpleasant things happened over there. But I didn't tell you the worst." He dropped his head, fear passing through his face. She took his hand to comfort him, but he pulled it away, certain her sympathy would disappear once he'd said it all.

"One night, three of my buddies and I were on patrol in this little town north of Mosul. We were mostly just out to make sure no one was going to try anything—like cops patrol to make their presence known. We'd had a couple beers and were laughing, telling jokes and such when we came around a corner and saw this woman turning down an alley. One of the guys tried to talk to her, but she didn't know much English. He kept on talking at her and then tried to pull off her hijab, saying something about wanting to see her hair."

Matt looked away, horror in his eyes as he remembered. Finally, he continued, but Nicole could tell he was reluctant to speak the full truth of the experience.

"Then he started putting his hands all over her. At first, we told him to back off, but when he didn't, one of the other guys tried to pull them apart and wound up groping her too. I'll skip the gory details. The three of them raped her. I never touched her, I froze, I mean really froze, but I didn't stop them, couldn't—there were three of them to one of me. And I watched. God, I watched. It was the most horrible thing I'd ever seen."

He broke then, head in hands, shoulders shaking. Nicole reached out and gently touched his arm, to bring him back.

"When it was over, we went back to the barracks, never talked about it again. Of course, none of us was ever the same after that. We stopped palling around. Couldn't stand to see each other, knowing what had happened. My tour was almost up then, and I found out a couple of weeks after I'd returned that an IED got them. Two died right away, and the other was paralyzed. I'm ashamed to admit it, but I was glad. They'd never be able to hurt anyone again. We'd never told anyone else about it, never owned up to it, or even tried to see what happened to the woman."

He stopped and looked cautiously at her to see how badly she was taking this. Her face was subdued but not withdrawn, so he continued.

"When I first came back, I tried to just forget it, pretend it hadn't happened. I told myself it was a fluke, a horrible thing in a horrible place, and I blamed the war for it. But I couldn't keep it down. The memory of certain...acts...would come up in my mind. If I saw a woman bend over...Just for a second, I could feel ME doing that to her, even though I didn't do it in Iraq. I could feel what it would be like to..."

He bowed his head and couldn't look at her. She could see he was in agony about this now. She didn't try to take his hand again, but she reached over and touched it lightly to let him know she was still with him. He broke again and cried, his whole body shaking with the emotion, the shame. She wanted desperately to hold him to her heart, so he could feel the compassion she had for him, but she knew he wouldn't be able to let it in yet. So she waited.

When the sobs finally subsided, she calmly spoke his name. "Matt."

He slowly lifted his head, afraid of what he would see in her eyes. He was shocked to see tenderness, and it made his tears flow again.

"I'm so sorry you had to go through all that. Do you think you can tell me about your dream now?" she said softly.

He hesitated, then almost in a whisper said, "The scenes change from dream to dream, but basically they're the same. I come up behind a woman and push her to the ground. Then I grab her hair and take her from behind, very forcefully. When I'm done, I snap her neck, killing her, and I move on."

When he finished, he sat for a long time with his head hung. He couldn't believe his own ears, that he'd actually spoken those words out loud. For the first time, ever, he had let it all out, and he was emotionally drained. He had told her, almost a stranger, the very worst of himself, and now there was nowhere, and nothing else, to hide. It was the most vulnerable he'd ever been. And as awful as it was, strangely, the feeling was cleansing. He waited in the stillness for her to speak, fully expecting her to tell him to leave.

"Can I tell you a story now?" she asked.

Surprised, he looked up at her and nodded slowly.

"Years ago, I kept hearing this story on the news about a guy who'd beaten a toddler to death. When the poor kid was examined, they found bruises all over him, many were weeks old. And X-rays showed he'd had multiple broken bones in his short life. This had all been going on for a long time. Made me sick to my stomach to hear it. And most of me was saying 'just kill that bastard.' But it also triggered something. A piece of me I didn't know I had inside started imagining how it would feel to so totally dominate another human being like that. How powerful it would make you feel to beat someone up, even a weakling. Of course, there were other voices in my head countering that only an extremely twisted and insecure person would even want to exert that kind of power over another. And not for a nanosecond do I actually think it's okay to beat a child, or rape a woman. Still, that piece found it all so exciting, like tapping into pure power. I can tell you it was pretty sobering to know there was something inside me so odious to the rest of me."

He stared at her, eyes wide. This sweet woman, beat up a helpless kid? He couldn't wrap his head around it. Even though she hadn't actually done it, just as he hadn't, the thought that she'd felt a part of her could, just as he did, sent him reeling.

"Matt, we all have many parts inside us, many of them very different than the others. There are 'child' parts who've never grown up and never will, that are still wounded by things that happened long ago, that can't handle the pressures of life adults have to deal with, that can only see life through very naive eyes. Even the parts that are older can have very different agendas for our lives. Like the piece of me that just wants to be free, to make love to whoever she wants at the time and then moves on to the next one. Then there's a piece who wants a committed relationship, to build a home and long-term life with a man. Both of these characters are quite strong in me, and believe me, the tensions between them have made my life pretty chaotic."

His eyes widened still as he listened to her words. He'd never thought about people having different parts of themselves before, just assumed he was all one person. That's why his dreams were so horrifying—he thought that was all there was to him, and he'd labeled himself a rapist even though he himself had never committed that terrible act against a real-life woman.

She searched his face carefully. Was he ready to hear more? She hoped so.

"And, yes, there's a small piece of me that for a very brief time showed me that it could delight in beating up a child. It has never even come close to happening in all the time I've spent with my sister's kids—and I watch them a *lot*—even when they're being complete shits. But I sincerely felt it that day, the feelings were...shall we say, authentic. So now I know

I have that piece in me, and there's nothing really to do except *know* it."

She reached out now and took his hand in hers. This time he didn't pull back, just looked at her in wonder. A tiny flicker of hope was growing in him, and he knew it was her doing.

"Do you think that's how it is with me?"

"Yes, Matt, I do. I think there is a piece of you that could relish raping a woman. But I think it's not really a part that you are supposed to play out in this life. You had the chance, back then, and your soul declined. This is kind of a gross way to say it, but the majority of the parts in you chose to be a spectator and not a participant in that situation. That means something, Matt. Please let that one in. You're not here on this planet to *do* that to a woman."

She had to stop. He was sobbing again.

The enormity of what she was saying was too much for him to bear. *I might not be the horrible monster I've been so afraid of. Can it be possible?*

Gently, she continued. "Matt, you don't always act on impulse, do you? When there's a slow driver in front of you, and you're in a hurry, you don't run them off the road, do you?" He shook his head. "You may have a thought of how satisfying it would be to shove that car out of your way, but you don't actually do it. What I'm getting at is that not all impulses have to be acted out. Things that certain pieces of ourselves want to express don't always have to be expressed outside of us. I think that's why you have these dreams—it gives that part of you a chance to express itself. Without needing to act out in reality. The dream itself balances your psyche."

She could see he was in emotional shock, rapidly going into

overload. And once people go there, nothing else can get in. So she stood up, went over to him and pulled him to his feet. Then she embraced him, with an open heart, as fully as she could. He didn't really respond, didn't put his arms around her, and she knew he didn't feel worthy of her compassion yet. Still she held him close, not letting him deny that she cared for him. When she could feel him begin to relax a bit, she said, "I think you could use some sleep now. Will you come back to bed with me?"

Not trusting himself to speak—he was so tied up in knots, full of despair, and somehow hope at the same time—he just nodded and followed her. He lay down, facing away from her with his knees almost up to his chest. She spooned behind him and, grateful, he moved back into her. *Different pieces, don't have to actually do that, nothing to do but know it.* The thoughts swirled in his head until they all blended together in a white mist.

They both slept peacefully until morning.

chapter 10

When he opened his eyes, there she was watching him. She smiled and touched his face gently with her fingers.

"How do you feel?" she asked.

He didn't answer at first. He didn't know how he felt. He wondered if last night had even been real. But there it was in her eyes, and finally, he managed to say he wasn't sure.

"Would you like to talk some more, or just be alone, or maybe do something simple like going into town for some breakfast?"

He nodded. "Food sounds wonderful." Her body was so close, so warm beside him that it was impossible not to think of how amazing dancing with her had been. Part of him so much wanted to make love to her, feel her again, but he knew he wasn't ready to be that close, to anyone really, just yet.

So they got dressed and drove into the small town just north of the campground. He was quiet and pensive on the way there, and she didn't press him to talk. He had a lot to process, needed a break from the intensity of the night before.

The restaurant was a typical small country café. She'd been there before, and though the furnishings were quite plain, the food was all homemade and delicious. She especially loved their blueberry pancakes. As they walked to the door, they saw a God Bless Our Troops sticker in the window, and she felt him flinch. *So much guilt this man carries.*

The place was busy, full of people chattering away, and it was nice to be in a simple, everyday atmosphere. They both relaxed as the waitress showed them to a table by the window.

"Oh man, what a view," he said as they sat down.

"I so love these mountains," she replied. "I grew up here in Wyoming and can't imagine living anywhere else."

"I can believe that. I've only been here a short while, and already I don't want to leave." He looked right at her as he said this, and she blushed. *Could he actually care for me?*

Breakfast was exactly what they'd both needed to bring them back into the normal here and now. She got her pancakes, with eggs, and he inhaled his plate of bacon, homemade hash browns and eggs. Through it all, they chatted casually about their families and their favorite things to do. When he found out she'd loved riding horses as a kid, he suggested they find someplace to ride later.

"Oh, I'd love to. But you have to promise me you'll wear a cowboy hat if we do. You'd look hot in a cowboy hat."

Now it was his turn to blush. "Well, ma'am. We'll have to find someplace to buy one. I left mine behind a couple lifetimes ago."

She giggled. He'd tried to say that with a southern drawl, but it was clear this Cali boy did not have it down.

When he paid the check, he asked the waitress where they could ride and where he could buy a hat. She gave them directions for both, and Nicole and Matt walked out, hand in hand.

They had to drive another fifteen miles to get to Colbran and Jack's Outdoors. She'd only been to the store once, but she knew they had everything cowboy. As they pulled into the parking lot, she looked coyly at Matt and said, "This is going to be fun."

The store was huge, and they just wandered around for a while. Nicole especially wanted to see what interesting new camping gear Jack's might have.

"Wow, look at this, Matt," she said, pointing to a sky chair with a stand. "Have you ever sat in a sky chair?"

"No. Seems kind of flimsy." He looked doubtfully at the canvas, bowl-shaped seat with wooden poles holding it in place.

"Oh, try it. This is a different version, but I had one once, with a much larger stand made of four by fours. After I put it up, I sat in it for three hours straight. They're great to read in, or nap in, or just veg."

Matt settled himself in the chair, leaning back with his hands behind his head as he felt it swinging gently beneath him.

"Yeah, I see what you mean. Maybe I'll just stay here while you go horseback riding." He grinned.

"As if! Get your butt out of there, and let's find you a hat."

They made their way to the clothing section. The first thing that caught her eye was a blue and yellow plaid western shirt with dark blue piping on the yoke.

"Matt, this would look divine on you. Please try it on?"

"You really trying to turn this Army guy into a cowboy?" he asked playfully.

"Well…if the boots fit," she said hopefully.

While he'd been in the dressing room, Nicole looked for a hat. She thought black might be too dark for him, and the lighter whites and beiges were a bit washed out. The one she liked best was light brown felt with a dark brown leather band decorated with inset diamond-shaped turquoise and silver studs.

Matt emerged from the dressing room *lookin' mighty fine*—lordy, she was even starting to think country.

"Wow, dude, that shirt is so you," she said, as she handed him the hat. As she'd thought, the shirt was incredible on his sculpted body. Her eyes traveled over his chest, his stomach. She could almost feel them beneath the material. The blue in the plaid matched the blue of his eyes and made them sparkle.

He put the hat on his head, settled it on at just the right angle and turned to look at her. He smiled when he saw the expression on her face, that slow boyish grin with just a touch of wickedness. She felt like she was melting at his feet.

"Okay," she squeaked. "I think that's the one."

He laughed, to see her so affected. As they stood in line to pay, he bent down and kissed her. *Ah, there's that fire in her eyes. I like that.*

chapter 11

They got to the stables fifteen minutes before their scheduled ride. A tall, lanky young man, in all-out cowpoke attire, introduced himself as the head trail guide, Michael. He asked Matt and Nicole to fill out the limitations of liability paperwork.

There were several others going on the ride with them. A mom in her thirties had two kids who were a real handful. Both boys, they were so excited they could hardly stand still. When Michael told them they had to leave their new cowboy hats behind to put on helmets, they were so disappointed.

Lucky that rule doesn't apply to adults. They'd have to fight me to get Matt's off. I could look at him in that hat all day, Nicole thought.

Then there was a teenager who introduced himself as Tom and said he was camping with his folks, but they hadn't wanted to ride, which was just fine with him. After all, what teenager wants to do stuff with his parents? He told the guide he'd taken lessons as a kid, so they gave him one of the taller mounts.

Another couple looked Middle Eastern. Both seemed nervous when the guide brought their horses out. They obviously hadn't ridden before. The woman had a hijab on, and Nicole watched Matt's face closely to see if he was having trouble being around her. His face was set, and his breathing shallow. He was struggling to contain his emotions. Fortunately, their horses arrived, and he had to focus on getting himself in the saddle. It was actually pretty cute watching this surfer dude try to get on the horse. Nicole had to put her hands over her mouth to keep from laughing out loud. *Guess some physical skills just don't transfer well to new challenges.*

When everyone was mounted, the second trail guide, Michelle, led them all to the path into the mountains. There was, of course, Michael in the rear as well. Nowadays, it was all walking, only on the path, the horses trained to do nothing else. Nicole remembered her days as a teenager and the stable she used to go to with her sister. They would get on the horses and head out to a field by themselves to do whatever they wanted. The pace was as fast as they could get the horses to go. Cantering was the best with that wonderful rocking motion, wind in the hair, and feeling the power of the animal underneath her. Nicole sighed.

Oh well, it was still nice to be in the saddle. And Matt looked so sexy in his new shirt and hat as he rode in front of her. Yeah, she could definitely handle the view of this strong yet fragile man. The conversations and events of the night before filled her head, and she marveled at the mystery that had brought them together at just this time in their lives. He was a soul struggling with the weight of aspects of himself he could not assimilate, and she—thanks to that conference—had been shown a way to see things from a deeper perspective, even though she was not yet able to fully love. Her heart swelled with gratitude for her teacher and compassion for Matt and herself.

They wound their way through some of the most beautiful mountain terrain Matt had ever seen, and Nicole could tell he was now relaxed and enjoying himself. Michael broke the silence frequently with chatter about the wildlife, the history of the area and various points of interest. As they approached a more open section of meadow by the trail, he asked everyone to keep an eye out for prairie dog holes. The colony had grown this year and increased their territory. Horses' legs and holes in the ground were not a good combination.

The two younger boys had trouble keeping their horses from stopping to munch on the grasses and bushes along the trail. Michael told them over and over to pull the reins up high to lift the horses' heads, then kick to get them moving again. Considering the kids' size relative to the mounts they were on, this was quite a job. Actually, Nicole thought they did pretty well. She'd seen grown men and women not be able to handle their horses as well as these two did.

The other riders chimed in from time to time, and it was clear that the Middle Eastern man couldn't speak much English, but the woman could. She seemed to be having fun and laughed often at things her husband was saying. Nicole found herself talking with her occasionally as she was just behind Nicole in the line.

They were just coming around a curve in the trail next to some tall bushes when Michelle's horse and the one the mother was riding spooked and started trotting quickly away, hooves pounding the earth. Michelle spurred her horse to the mother's and grabbed the reins before he could run off with her. At that moment, an elk popped out of the bushes, and everyone watched in amazement as he bounded off across the meadow. Michael said that was the first one he'd seen up there that season. They were lucky to have caught such a magnificent sighting.

When they all returned to the stables and had dismounted and turned in the horses, the Middle Eastern woman, Shatha, asked Nicole if maybe she and Matt might like to join them for lunch nearby. Nicole could see that Matt was pretty uncomfortable with the idea, but she quickly answered yes. She had a feeling it would be good, be healing, for Matt to be with them.

They followed the couple's car to a cute little café about three miles up the road. Matt was pretty much silent on the way, and Nicole let him deal with his feelings.

After the hostess had seated them at the table, they all introduced themselves. Jamali and Shatha had just come to the US a few months ago from Iraq. He was an accountant, she a housewife who'd done some studying on her own time. She'd taught herself English. Their kids had come over to attend colleges in the States, and the oldest had finally gotten settled enough to bring over his parents, after slogging through years of immigration paperwork. As they talked, Nicole could see the tension and uncertainty building in Matt's face. So she decided to face them head-on.

"Matt here was in the Army, stationed in Iraq for a while."

She saw his face turn white as a sheet, his eyes in fight or flight mode.

"Oh, that is so wonderful," Shatha said. "We have so much to thank you for. Where were you?"

"Mostly north of Mosul," Matt just managed to get out.

"We lived south of there, about two hundred kilometers. There was not as much fighting where we were, but there was always the danger of a sniper, and more if the war moved closer. It was comforting to know you soldiers were there to protect us from the Al Qaeda forces. We know a lot of you sacrificed much for us."

The pain on Matt's face was almost too much for Nicole to bear. Jamali and Shatha didn't seem to notice, but she could tell he was in a fierce struggle of conflicting emotions. The praise he was hearing for having served just could not overcome the torture of what he'd seen his buddies do, and what he still dreamed about.

"Yes, they did," Nicole said. "As necessary as it can sometimes be, war is a horrific thing. So many terrible things happen in war."

"Oh, that is so true," Shatha said. "Soldiers seem to become different people somehow. They have to. They protect, but they also have to kill, and it was very hard on them. To be one thing and yet another at the same time. I know that some did really bad things. I heard many stories, but I always felt so sorry for them."

She looked directly at Matt then. "All of you were so far from home, fighting for people you had never even met, for some abstract thing you call freedom. And you were in constant fear for your own lives. I cannot even imagine what pressure that must have been for you."

Matt was staring open-mouthed, trying desperately to hide what was going on inside him. He could not believe what he was hearing in Shatha's voice—compassion. Nicole reached under the table to hold his hand, then she said, "I'm so glad to hear you say that, Shatha. I wish more of our soldiers could hear it."

She knew Matt needed time to let this conversation in. So she did a one-eighty and asked Jamali and Shatha about how they felt about leaving Iraq.

"As delighted as you must be to be near your kids now, it surely was difficult leaving your home."

"Yes, it was. We still have many relatives in Iraq that we will probably never see again. I cannot pretend that is not hard." Her eyes got misty, but she braved on. "It has been quite an experience, adjusting to your culture, which is so different from ours. Jamali and I are not so deeply dedicated to Islam as many in our country are, but the lack of connection to what you call God here seems to have left many people, what shall I say, lost."

"That's true, there are a lot of us here who don't have much connection to anything other than our own little lives. But while so many have left the churches, there is also a growing number who have found their own connection to…some still say God, others just call it the Divine, or Source, or Life with a capital L."

Shatha paused for a minute, then said, "Yes, you Americans really like your independence and individualism. It is your weakness and your strength. It keeps you separate from each other, makes you…'go it alone' I heard someone say once. And, it also means you try to honor each person. Especially women. I do get bad stares sometimes, wearing the hijab, but mostly I get treated like a human equal to every other. In Iraq, there are so many things a woman cannot do. I am discovering that driving a car to the store by myself is fun."

"I'm glad you're getting to experience that equality here," Nicole said. "We don't always get it right, but like you said, we do try."

Shatha paused, peered thoughtfully at Nicole and Matt, and said, "I do wish Americans would try to understand us better. So many seem to think that because I wear the hijab, I am being bullied or shamed by my husband and the Imam. It is not true. I choose to wear it as a symbol of my faith and as an expression of modesty and devotion. I am not forced." She looked at Jamali, who took her hand. They smiled lovingly at each other.

"I understand, Shatha," said Nicole. "I wish the same thing. People can be so quick to judge, especially when it's someone who is different from them."

Nicole turned the conversation to Iraq's rich history then, hoping to pull Matt in. And it worked. With just a few probing questions, she managed to draw him out, and soon he was discussing history and even politics with her and Shatha. They got Jamali to chime in from time to time too. By the time the meal was finished, Matt seemed himself again.

As they walked out the door, Shatha thanked them for joining her and Jamali for lunch and said how happy she was to have met Matt and Nicole. Matt was surprised when she boldly reached out her hand to shake his. It wasn't customary in Iraq for a woman to touch a man in public, even her own husband. It was a gesture that showed respect, an American gesture.

Nicole sensed his hesitation, before he responded in kind. His eyes flashed fear again, just for a second. Nicole shook Shatha's and Jamali's hands and wished them both well. They all said their goodbyes and went their separate ways.

chapter 12

As *they pulled up to the camper*, Nicole asked, "Want to come in for a drink?"

"Sure, maybe another margarita?"

They went inside the camper, and he watched her as she fixed a margi for him and a gin and tonic for herself. They raised their glasses in a toast, then she reached out and ran her hand down his chest. He flinched.

"Aren't you afraid I'll hurt you now? After all I've told you?"

She looked at him, straight into his doubtful eyes.

"No, Matt. I'm not. And I'll tell you why. Twice already I've seen, well, felt really," she said, grinning, "how you are when you make love to a woman. The part you're so afraid of is not in play, not on the stage so to speak, during the physical act in real life."

"So far, that's been true. But it could come out any time, couldn't it?"

"I honestly don't think so, for you. I had a man in my life once who was capable of being hurtful to a woman. In fact, he hurt me, and later another woman."

Her eyes went dark, as she remembered.

"There was always this undercurrent to him. I'd be hard-pressed to put my finger on exactly what I mean, in the way of specifics. You know how sometimes you can just *feel* another person, energetically. Deep down, I knew he couldn't be trusted, that there was something sinister inside him, something that was unsafe for me. I do not feel that with you. Yes, you told me something you think is awful about yourself. But that's just a small part of you, a part that doesn't seem to want to express itself outside dreams."

He just looked at her, uncertainty in his eyes, along with the deep shame he felt.

"Matt, let me just be blunt here. You were a soldier, strong, and trained to kill, in certain situations. You're also a tender, loving man, who makes love with a gentle touch and manly force. But not brute force. You've never treated me with anything other than respect. This is who you are for me."

Tears sprang to his eyes, and she again reached out to hold him.

"I have no more reason to fear you than children had to fear me when I found that small part of me that could beat a child. Acting those things out in real life is just not in the cards for either of us."

The tears flowed freely now, in huge racking sobs as years of self-loathing began to release. She held him to her heart and stroked his hair. When he finally calmed down a bit, she kissed his forehead and gently lifted his chin so he could look into her eyes. They gazed at each other for a long time, seeing deeply soul to soul.

Tentatively, he kissed her. Softly at first, then more and more passionately as the feelings spread, and his arms wrapped around her in the most intimate embrace he'd ever felt. His full being entwined with her whole being.

Still wrapped up in their embrace, he asked her if they could put on some music and dance. He wanted time to let these new emotions settle in. So Nicole found her dance playlist on the iPod, and they began to move.

As he held her close, hips swaying in time to the music, Matt let himself fully feel his manhood for the first time since he'd returned from Iraq. He felt how his muscles moved, felt the strength in them, felt his feet firmly on the floor—so sure-footed and grounded in the earth. He felt his hands roaming gently over Nicole's body, back, hips and breasts. He felt how much he wanted this woman, to lie beside her, be inside her, rocking them both to that final moment of bliss. Momentarily, the dream came back to him, but now it somehow felt distant, like a receding memory. And it disappeared completely when he kissed Nicole tenderly.

She could feel his energy shifting, feel him coming back to himself, so she contented herself with the dancing. *Yes, I know you want to get him to that bed over there, but we have to be patient here*. She stroked his chest, his hips, and kissed him softly on his neck.

It had been so long since he'd let a woman's touch in, but now he felt every one of her caresses. In amazement, he felt the caring in her fingertips, the caring genuinely meant for him. The thought that he might be worthy of her love almost brought him to tears again, but the physical feelings were stronger now, and he really wanted her. He danced them closer to the bed, both of them shedding clothing as they went. When they reached it, she held his face in her hands, again looking deeply into his eyes.

"Make love to me, Matt," she said softly.

And he did.

chapter 13

As she'd hoped, an afternoon thunderstorm had settled in over them. Nicole snuggled in Matt's arms, and the gentle sound of the raindrops hitting the canvas over their heads nearly put them to sleep. It was a camper's lullaby.

Matt broke the spell. All their activity had worked up an appetite.

They decided to just eat a mix of whatever each of them had brought up—an odd dinner, but delicious. Matt had an assortment of canned vegetables, and Nicole had some Zuppa Toscana. They heated it all up on the camper's stove then sat down inside, still listening to the rain softly falling.

Their conversation was light chitchat while they ate. Nicole could see in his eyes that there was a lot of churning going on inside him. Things had moved at nearly the speed of light in the short time she'd known him. She hoped she hadn't pushed him too fast. It was clear that he'd never been exposed to some of the ideas she'd brought up.

After they ate, Nicole cleaned up while Matt made a roaring fire. The rain had stopped a short while ago. They got another drink and sat down in the camp chairs.

"Great fire, Matt."

"I love fires. Such a mystery—how it all burns. And the dancing flames are so mesmerizing."

"No kidding. I can watch a fire for hours. Such a peaceful time to just let the mind wander wherever it will."

He looked so relaxed, so serene, sitting there. They were silent for a while, then he said, "I really love being with you, Nicole. You have a way of making me feel like, well, me, but *all* of me. You know my worst secrets, and yet you somehow still accept me. I don't know how you do that."

"It can be very freeing to be fully seen by another human being, Matt. I just see you for what you are."

"You really do." He peered at her intently. "How come you know so much? I've never met anyone who can see things the way you do."

"Remember when I told you I went to a spiritual conference after my divorce? The teacher, and the group of people who were there, were completely amazing. They opened my eyes to perspectives I'd never even thought of before. Like that we all have different pieces inside us. That dreams can be all the expression a part needs to be satisfied. And so much more."

"Wow. I'm in awe. I can't believe how lucky I am to have met you," he said.

She blushed. "Well, the feeling is mutual. Can I ask you a question?"

"Of course."

"Have you told Amanda about your experience in Iraq? About your dreams?"

He hung his head and didn't speak for a minute.

"No. She's such a sweet, delicate person. I just couldn't bear to bring all that horrible stuff into her world. I know she wanted me to talk to her. She kept asking about Iraq and how it was for me over there. But I couldn't do it. That's one of the reasons she left."

"What were the other reasons?"

His shoulders sagged, and he looked at her mournfully.

"Matt, tell me if I'm being too nosy here."

"You're not. I think I need to get all this out. It's just hard..."

"I know—take your time."

"The not talking to her was bad enough. I know it hurt her a lot that I shut her out of that part of my life. But what was worse was that I couldn't make love to her anymore. Every time we would start, I would see that poor Iraqi woman. And I would push Amanda away."

The pain was too strong to speak now, and Nicole held his hand until he could go on.

"She was so patient with me, tried to talk to me about it, kept asking what was wrong. I made stuff up—told her I was tired, or not feeling good. But she knew I wasn't telling her the truth. I think she started to feel like there was something wrong with her, something I didn't like anymore. Which was so not true. I could see her withdrawing from me, see the hurt in her eyes, and one day she just stopped trying."

"Matt..."

"Sometimes, I would have those dreams, basically wake up screaming. It scared her to death. Especially since I couldn't tell her what they were." He gripped her hand tighter. "She tried, so hard. But finally, she just couldn't take it anymore. She had to leave."

He was broken now, and Nicole could see how much he still yearned for his ex-wife. Softly, she said, "I'm so sorry, Matt. It sounds to me like you both loved each other very much."

He nodded. "I'd do anything to get her back."

"Do you think, after everything that's happened up here, that you might be able to tell her about it now?"

His head snapped up, and he looked at her in amazement.

"Seriously? How could I explain all of this?" He pointed a finger at her then at him and back to her again. "No way. She wouldn't sit still long enough for me to get it all out. She's not going to see the rape and the dreams the way you do. I've never met anyone like you, able to handle what I've told you. She'd just bolt."

"Perhaps you're not giving her enough credit. She really wanted you to talk, to share. Surely she knew that whatever happened for you in Iraq wasn't pleasant. And that it would be about some horrific things. War is not nice. Yet she was asking, to know. She wanted to know you, all of you."

She raised her eyebrows and gave him a quizzical look that invited him to rethink.

"I guess that's true. But Nicole, it's one thing to tell someone about something terrible like you see on the news all the time, and another to tell something you yourself did. She would just see me as a monster. Never want to be with me again."

"You don't know that. It may seem likely, but honestly, you never gave her a chance, did you."

"Well, no." He dropped his head and sighed. "I just assumed..."

"Look, I'm not pushing for anything here. I mean, this is your life. I'll just say that if it were me in Amanda's place, I would want you to tell me. Even the really awful stuff. That's the only way I'd ever know if we could still work. I wouldn't be able to decide whether or not I could handle it without knowing what it was. Do you see my point? You put her in a position of not even being able to choose."

"I know, you're right. I was just too ashamed."

"Have you talked to her since the divorce?"

"Once or twice, to get things settled. But not really *talked.* She gets that sad look in her eyes, me too, and we just can't seem to go any further."

"Well, it's true, you can't. Not until that wall you built up is taken down. Matt, there's no two ways about it, you would have to get very vulnerable to tell her about everything, and there's certainly no guarantee that you'd like the outcome. But I look at you, feel you, and it's so clear how much you love this woman, how much you want Amanda in your life. And from what you've told me, she really loved you too. Aren't the two of you worth taking a chance on?"

He was silent for a while, letting it sink in. The thought of saying the awful words to Amanda scared him to death, but the truth of what Nicole was saying couldn't be denied.

"You're right, of course. It's going to take all the courage I ever had in my whole life, including in Iraq, and then some, to be able to tell her."

"Then let's toast to courage."

They clinked their glasses solemnly. Nicole fervently hoped that Matt and Amanda could find their way through.

chapter 14

The fire had mostly gone out while they were talking, and Nicole was unsure what would happen next. Considering the fact that Matt was still so in love with his ex-wife, would he still want to be with her, make love with her? Or was that part of their relationship, such as it was, over now? He was going back to Amanda—that was obvious—but she would have liked to spend this last night together. It was up to him though, and she waited until he made his intentions and desires clear.

He didn't move or speak for what seemed like forever. So much had happened in such a short time—this woman, the talks, the acceptance of him, the sex (*oh yes, surprisingly, the sex*), this new possibility of bringing Amanda back into his life. His head spun; he felt as though if he looked up at the stars, they would swirl madly around him. And he had to leave tomorrow. Tonight was his last chance to be with Nicole. He flashed on how it was to kiss her, hold her, be inside her. Being with her felt so freeing, so comfortable. But Amanda, who he would love forever…The conflict inside was crippling. He wished he could just flip a coin and be spared from making a decision.

It was the joyful sound of laughter from a campsite down the creek that threw him where he really wanted to be. In this special moment in time, Nicole. He stood up and pulled her to her feet, kissed her passionately. *Oh yes, I want you woman.* Her response to his kiss, her hungry mouth on his, told him she felt it too. Bodies on fire, they pressed against each other as though every minute could be their last. Their hands groped, roaming over stomachs, thighs and breasts. When he felt her hand moving to more private parts, Matt broke away, chuckling.

"Maybe we should go inside?"

They quickly stowed the camp chairs, gathered the few remaining items on the table and entered the camper.

Nicole had just drawn the last curtain when she turned around to see Matt standing still, staring intently at her. His expression of tenderness, lust and urgency sent tingles of energy through every fiber of her being. Fully aware of how precious this man was to her, she moved slowly toward him and put her hand over his heart. He shuddered with the intensity of the feeling of her heart energy flowing to his. Holding her with his eyes, he took her hand and kissed her palm softly. Then he gently flicked his tongue in her palm and took one finger in his mouth as he unbuttoned her blouse with his other hand. Her desire for him leapt. With her free hand, she unzipped his jeans, pushed them to the floor. Slowly, deliberately, they undressed each other, never breaking eye contact.

They stood for a moment, naked, not touching, connecting energetically. Finally, she could stand it no more—she wanted him as badly as she had wanted anything in her life—and she grabbed his hips and pulled him inside her. The feeling of him filling her was exquisite; the feeling of her enclosing him was utterly divine. He drove into her again and again until they found their release.

She wanted to tell him how incredible he was, but she was beyond words. She held him close, stroked his chest, kissed him softly. He ran his hand slowly down her back to her hips, kept her pressed to him. Neither wanted to let the other go. She reached up to touch his cheek and felt his tears.

"Oh, Matt."

"Nicole." He could barely speak. "How can I ever tell you how much you've meant to me?"

"Dear sweet man, you just did, making love to me. No words could say more than that."

He nodded, kissed her cheek, her eyes, her lips. They caressed each other tenderly, until they fell asleep.

When they woke in the morning, they lay a long time in each other's arms, both dreading what was to come. He gently moved his fingers over her body as she looked deep into his eyes. God, she was going to miss those expressive, blue eyes. It's said that the eyes are the windows to the soul, and she felt it keenly, the soul of him. She ran her hand through his hair, pulling his head to hers, and kissed him softly. Slowly, savoring every touch, every moment, they made love, and when at last he left her body, she cried.

chapter 15

He packed up his camping gear and cleaned up the campsite while she got her shower and made some breakfast. Both of them tried to keep it light while they ate, knowing that if they didn't, the parting would be too hard.

"So, where are you headed now?"

"Well, I'm going to spend a couple days in Yellowstone, see Old Faithful and all. Then I work my way back home through Idaho, Salt Lake City, and such."

"That's going to be a nice trip, Matt. Yellowstone is seriously cool. You know there's a volcano underneath that is overdue to explode."

"Really? I didn't know that."

"Yeah, and apparently if it really blows, it will blanket most of North America in ash. Would kind of make the 'big one' along California seem minor."

"Are they thinking it will happen soon? Maybe you should move."

She laughed. "They don't know. And I don't know that moving would do much good, as big as the thing is. I figure life's harsh, this is a violent planet I'm living on, and if life wants to take me out, well, who am I to say no?"

"Guess that's one way to look at it. Me, I'd be kind of freaked out living so close to that. But then I live close to the fault, so what the hell. Just what you're used to, I suppose."

"Have you ever been in a strong earthquake? I think that would be so odd, having the earth shake underneath you."

He stood up and started jumping around in the camper. It rocked back and forth as he landed. He grinned and said, "Feels like this."

Both of them broke out laughing. It was just what they needed, to help diffuse the heaviness of their last morning. They cleaned up the dishes together, chatting all the while. When there was nothing left to do, Matt pulled her close and kissed her softly on the lips.

"Nicole, I can't even begin to know how to thank you. I was so broken when I came up here, and now I feel like there might be hope after all." Gratitude filled his eyes as they looked deeply into hers. "You're a very special woman, Nicole."

"And you're a very special, very good man, Matt. I truly mean that. I hope with all my heart that you can find the courage to talk to Amanda. You belong with her."

She struggled to say those last words, pushing him to another woman. But however much she cared about Matt, however close they'd been, she'd sensed from the beginning that they wouldn't last.

"I hope so too, and I'll be working on that all the way home. There's a lot to think about."

He turned around, opened the door to the camper and paused. It was so hard to leave this woman, to say a final goodbye to someone who had changed his life in the most miraculous way. *Talk about needing courage; leaving you is tearing me up*. He took in a deep breath and stepped out. She followed, and they stood silent for a long time, drinking in the sight of each other.

Then he gave her one of the boyish grins she loved so much, turned around, and was gone.

chapter
16

Nicole moped around the campground for several hours after he left. As much as she usually loved being up here alone, with Matt gone it suddenly felt lonely and empty. Even walking to the river, her favorite nature setting, the place that always calmed her heart no matter what, didn't help. Clearly, peace was no longer in the cards here, so she decided to just cut the trip short. She packed up quickly and left.

Walking through the door of her home, she was struck with how odd the reentry felt. Her gaze fell on the plush green couch in the living room, family pictures on the wall, and the soft rose carpeting. Stairs leading up to the bedrooms, the hall to her craftsman style kitchen. The dining table of warm cherry wood, chairs covered in fabric reminiscent of peacock feathers. She'd lived here for years, and it was all so familiar, yet strangely new too. Camping does that to you. For a brief time, you live in an alternate reality, and when you return, it is as though you've just stepped back out of a dream. And this time, it was an especially vivid Matt dream.

Unpacking could wait, she decided as she opened her laptop to check email. Sure enough, there was one from Sam about the wedding for Hayley and Mark. She had been basking in the glow of her time with Matt all the way down the mountain. Even sad thoughts that she'd never see him again couldn't overcome the joy at how special their connection had been. Now she sighed. Here was real life again.

Going through the mail was always a chore—so much junk. *Ah yes, but think about how many jobs are supported by all that crap*. She did three loads of wash while she took stock of what food there was in the house and made a grocery list. Shopping would have to come later though. She needed to concentrate on the work Sam's message outlined.

The event would certainly be an interesting one, the clients being who they were, and she was quickly absorbed in it. Hayley Ross and Mark Harrison were both star country singers constantly in the papers, as they were madly in love and had met while both were married to someone else. Now that their respective divorces had been finalized, they were free to get "hitched" like Hayley's last song said. As burned as they'd been in the press lately, they weren't about to risk a large Hollywood- or Nashville-style wedding. They wanted something small, but still nice, in a relatively out-of-the-way place—Cheyenne, where they'd met. So everything was to be hush-hush. Nicole read through what Sam had sent, then called him to come over, so they could start hashing out a plan for their presentation to the couple.

When Sam walked in, Nicole studied him as she hadn't in a long time. With a tall, solid body, nicely tanned skin, dark brown hair, and soft brown eyes rimmed by long, straight lashes, he was decidedly handsome. And such a teddy bear—the kind of guy you just wanted to hug tight and cuddle with. No wonder women threw themselves at him. Except the one woman he'd always wanted—her. She'd loved him so much once. Why did she keep pushing him away? And how in the world was she going to tell him about Matt?

"Hey girl, how was your camping trip? Back kind of early, aren't you?" Sam said, while giving her his big bear hug.

"Pretty interesting actually. And unexpected." She sat down and fidgeted with a length of purple ribbon on the desk, trying to drum up some courage. "I met someone."

She hated saying this, but they'd always told each other about people in their lives. They were best friends, didn't hold things back. No matter how uncomfortable it made him, he'd made it clear he wanted to know.

Sam's face fell as he slumped into a chair.

"This guy camping in the space next to mine. Matt. From San Diego. It was…intense."

She hardly dared look at him, knowing how much this would hurt him. She hoped he wouldn't ask for details as he always did when she'd been with others before. This time it would just be too hard to say the words. Especially since there was so much of Matt's story she could not reveal.

Sam sat in stunned silence, trying to grasp the significance of this particular development in light of all their history. The tone in her voice said this had been no quick fling. Just how serious was she about this man?

And was their history going to ever turn his way again?

So much hinged on their chemistry—had started with chemistry.

Born and raised in massively dynamic Jefferson City, Missouri, and one of six kids, he'd been dying to leave home since early high school. For his twelfth birthday, he'd gotten a chemistry set, and he loved mixing things, watching the reactions of this blending with that. One day, Sam was in the kitchen while his mom baked bread, and he realized that cooking was really just a more artful, and delicious, form of chemistry. Intrigued, he began making all sorts of extraordinary dishes for the family meals and discovered how much pleasure his cooking gave to people. His mom loved it. His father did not. Cooking was for women in his father's eyes, and the disapproval drove Sam away.

For some inexplicable reason, Wyoming sounded very exotic, all Western, cowboy, wide-open spaces. So after a couple of years in culinary school, he took a job with Cheyenne Frontier Days, and that's where he'd met Nicole. She was sitting on the front row in the first staff meeting, and the sight of her took his breath away. Dressed in bell-bottomed jeans and a light blue halter-top that matched the blue of her large eyes, she'd put her long, light brown hair in braids that day, giving her an air of infectious casualness. He was hooked, hard, and had been ever since.

He thought back to when she'd ended their months of love, the kind of love relationship he'd always dreamed of, so wanted again with her. He remembered the one word that kept him hanging on—"maybe."

"Please tell me you're just needing a break, that you'll come back to me. That we can be friends only for now, but someday we'll be more again."

"Maybe. I don't know. Sam, I can't promise more than that now. Maybe..."

He was still waiting. And he still had the ring.

But now here she was, attached to some random guy again. Another guy who wasn't him.

"Jesus, Nicole."

The utter dejection in his voice made Nicole wince.

"He's gone back home, and I don't know if I'll ever see him again. There are no plans," she said lamely.

"Is that why you're home early? He left, so you left?"

"Yeah, pretty much."

There was nothing she could say to ease his pain. Finally, he scraped his chair back and stood up. "I can't work with you on this wedding thing right now. I'll call you later."

He gave her a long, suffering look, and left.

chapter 17

"*Hey sis. Didn't expect to hear from you* till you came down from the hills." Jen sounded surprised and pleased to hear Nicole's voice.

"Hi, Jen. I'm down. Cut the camping short."

"What happened? You usually love being up there alone."

"Well…I met an amazing guy. He was in the campsite next to mine. Yummy with a spoon. We had a good time, and when he left, it suddenly felt kind of lonely. Plus, Sam has a potential new client. So I came down early."

"Oh my God, a new guy. Spill the beans, girl."

"Don't get too excited. It was definitely hot and heavy while he was there, but he lives in San Diego, and I doubt I'll ever see him again."

"What, like you can't visit each other?"

"Not likely. We talked a lot, a *lot* actually, and it's pretty clear he still loves his ex-wife. So even if we were in the same town, there wouldn't be much chance of a future there."

"That's too bad. Or is it?"

"Yes and no. I think it's going to be one of those 'flash of bright light' times in my life. You know, here today, gone tomorrow. Wonderful while it lasted," Nicole said wistfully.

"Damn, wish I could have met him. He sounds interesting."

"Oh, he definitely was. In a lot of ways. Sex was incredible. We talked, deep. Instant connection. Like that." Nicole sighed. "Kind of wish you could have met him too. He's a good guy."

"So, are you going to tell Sam?" Nicole could hear the worry in Jen's voice as she said this.

"Already did. He came over to talk about the new client and of course asked about camping. I can't lie to him. He's my best friend, besides you, and he always says he wants to know. He wasn't too happy."

"I bet. I promise not to lecture you again, but I really like Sam, and you know I've always wished you two would get together for real. I remember how happy you were for a time there, and I've never really understood why you broke it off. It pains me to see him hurt so much when you hook up with someone else. Especially since you have this wonderful, devoted man just waiting for you to see the light and let him back in."

Jen could almost see Nicole grimace over the phone. "God, Jen, I know. I just can't seem to crack this thing, this wall inside that stops me."

"Well, if there's anything I can do…"

"Yeah, I'd let you know. Listen, Jen, I gotta go. Just got back, and there's so much to do."

"Okay, see you later. Let's do lunch soon."

"Sounds good. I'll call you. Bye."

Jen sighed sympathetically. "Bye, little sis."

chapter 18

Nicole was knee-deep in the wedding venue search, just two weeks after her camping trip, when Matt called. It was quite the jolt as she'd tried hard to keep him out of her mind since their time together, tried to let him go. *He belongs to Amanda, you know.*

"Nicole, please, can I talk to you? I had that dream again last night, and I can't shake it. I remember everything you said, I really do, but I didn't expect that stuff to come back. I'm at my wits' end."

"Matt, of course, you can talk to me. It's really great to hear your voice." She tried to get him to relax a bit. "Being with you camping was wonderful, getting to know you, the horseback riding, all our talks, and, well, you know." She chuckled a little.

Her soothing voice calmed him. "Oh, Nicole, it's so nice to be talking to you too." Matt paused. "What am I going to do about these dreams? They rattle me horribly."

"Well, let's work with this. Apparently, this part of you—and remember it's a small part—is still needing to express itself or at least be seen. Have you made any progress with the acceptance of this part?"

"No, not really. It's hard, going back and reliving what happened in Iraq." He sounded exasperated. "To most of me, that's just *wrong*, which leaves me no way to see that part of myself as anything other than something that really should not be there."

"Matt, the only way you can accept a part like this is to seriously expand your view of what life is. Life has bigger ideas of what it wants than we mortals can fathom. Human beings are finite, so we fear death and pain, and we have our preferences of how we want things to be. Life, you know the one with the capital L, is infinite, so even the things we think are so awful are but the blink of an eye in its grand scheme. And even the pain we experience as humans is a valuable experience to Life, to whom it's just a fleeting blip. If I were in your shoes, I would just try to grasp the concept that whatever made you did not make a mistake. This piece is in you for some reason that serves Life, even if it doesn't feel like it serves you as you know yourself. You may never understand it. Good grief, how could you really, but that doesn't mean it's *wrong*. Life doesn't work in terms of right and wrong like us short-term humans do. For you a key thing here is that this part is satisfied with just being in your dreams. You aren't being asked to actually do this. Do you think you could accept that Life knew what it was doing when it made you this way?"

He struggled to understand.

"Crap, that's hard. Growing up, I always heard the opposite from church, and really everyone. Such stuff is a *sin*, and you'll go to hell and all that. Even if it's just in your head. So no, I don't think I really can."

"Okay, let's start further back. Do you agree that whatever made you knows a heck of a lot more than you do?"

"Yesss..."

"So something that intelligent probably knows what it's doing?"

"Okay..."

"And you're second-guessing that intelligence, telling it that it made a mistake making you the way you are."

Matt squirmed in his chair. "Uh..."

"Kind of arrogant, when you really think about it. Just because it's not how you think you want to be, and it's uncomfortable because it's not okay in most people's eyes, you're essentially flipping the bird at Life when you don't accept yourself as you are."

"Damn, I hadn't thought of it that way. Really turns things around. I can almost get it..."

"Hard though isn't it? We're taught the 'this is right and that is wrong' so constantly that our preferences for this over that don't change easily. You have to leave that point of view behind and look at it all from a much, much broader view. A long-term view that knows eternity and oneness. Impossible for the human brain to grasp. I certainly can't. All I can do is catch a glimpse. So when I come up against something like what you're experiencing that is so out of whack with who my ego thinks it wants to be, I ask this question—why would Life want this, how does it serve?"

Her question shocked him, and he drew in his breath sharply. "How does it serve? I can't see that it serves me—it scares the hell out of me. What do you mean?"

She looked out her window, at the view of the mountains, like the ones near the campground where they'd met.

"Matt, you're looking at it from the smaller point of view, from your human eyes, not Life's eyes. I believe one way it serves, in you, is that the Iraq experience and dreams have made you much more aware of how abusive that kind of power can be. That's a core piece of rape—the power over another human being, just like the guy I told you about who beat the kid. And knowing you have that piece in you serves as a constant reminder to not go there. Truly, it makes you more gentle and loving. Still strong—I remember those muscles! But not a brute. Can you start to feel this?"

"Just barely." He paused, trying hard to grasp what she was saying. Feeling helpless, he said, "Nicole, what I'm really feeling is that I want to see you again, be with you again. It's like I can't feel what you're saying over the phone, not like when we're together. Would that even be possible?"

She was surprised by his question. She knew he still loved Amanda, wanted to go back to her. She'd mostly accepted that and had thought she would not see him again.

"Um, what did you have in mind?"

"Could I come to Cheyenne, like maybe for a weekend? Would that be too much trouble? Would you even want to see me?"

"Well, sure, it would be great to see you again. When?"

They talked dates, made a plan for him to come to Cheyenne in a week. When they got off the phone, Nicole wondered how it would be to be with him again. *Nice, very nice.*

Her spirits fell quickly as she remembered that would be the weekend of the rafting trip with Sam.

chapter 19

Today was a big day. Hayley Ross, Mark Harrison, and Hayley's agent, Ginger, were coming to town to see what Sam and Nicole had in mind for their "perfect Western wedding."

As soon as she had returned from her camping trip with Matt, Nicole had bought all of Hayley's and Mark's CDs. She'd been listening to their music while she worked ever since. In fact, several of the ideas for the wedding plans had come from their songs.

Sam would pick them up from the airport and be at her place around 1:30 p.m. Nicole had spent the morning cleaning house. The closets were full of stuff quickly stashed. While she tidied up, Sam had made appetizer samplers. All in all, they were both a little anxious. This kind of exposure could bring them a ton of business, once the wedding was over and it hit the news.

The last week had been a whirlwind of preparation. Sam seemed to have finally stopped moping about Matt, settling back into the familiar routine of partnership. She'd checked out a half-dozen potential venues, everything from hotels to dude ranches. Actually, the dude ranch seemed to be the best fit. It was far enough out of town to keep Hayley and Mark's privacy easily guarded, and she had liked the owners immediately when she spoke to them on the phone. The ranch, in the McGill family for generations, had that old-time charm yet was tastefully updated with all the modern conveniences. Plenty of cabins and lodge rooms were available to house the couple's guests. Nicole hoped they would like the place as much as she had. She'd put together the usual picture board with all the possibilities for them to choose from, but studying it, it was obvious the dude ranch was her favored venue.

Sam's SUV pulled into the drive. Nicole smoothed the freshly ironed pink and white checked blouse she was wearing with her blue jeans and took a deep breath. *Here we go.*

In walked a couple custom designed for the front pages. Hayley was tiny compared to the tall cowboy next to her, but energetically she certainly held her own. Her long, dark hair, tanned skin, and flouncy dress made a delightful contrast to his blond hair, stubble of a beard and tight jeans. *They look like a lot of fun,* thought Nicole.

"Hi. Welcome to Cheyenne. I'm Nicole, and it's very nice to meet you Hayley, Mark, Ginger."

Did she imagine that Ginger gave her a more piercing look than the others? She remembered that Sam had worked with her some years ago, and Nicole briefly questioned just what their relationship might have been.

She shook hands with each as they came in. Sam was last, and she gave him a "holy cow, I hope this goes well" smile as he brushed by her. He squeezed her arm reassuringly.

"Please sit down." She gestured at the couch and living room chairs. "Would anyone like something to drink? I have iced tea, lemonade, soft drinks..."

Nicole got glasses for everyone while Sam brought in the appetizers.

"These are just a few examples of what we might serve as starters for your wedding," he said as he offered the tray to each guest. Hayley took a bite of the salmon crostini, and beamed.

"Wow, that's incredible. Mark, you gotta try one of these."

"Yeah, I will. And you need to try these. Man, this is just what we were hoping for." Mark shoved another of the ham and goat gouda gougères into his mouth.

As they tried each of the appetizers, sipped their drinks, and made the usual small talk, it became clear to both Sam and Nicole that these people were down to earth good folk who'd be a blast to work with. By the time Nicole brought out the picture board to get to business, she felt like they'd been friends for quite some time.

Actually, Sam and Ginger sort of were, and as Nicole watched him playfully touch Ginger's arm, Nicole wondered again if they'd been more than just friends. She was surprised to feel a small stab of jealousy and immediately pushed the thought out of her head.

Nicole began the pitch with the venues. When she described the dude ranch, Hayley clapped her hands excitedly.

"When can we go see it?"

Nicole grinned, happy to please her client.

"We have an appointment to visit at three this afternoon."

They talked in broad strokes about Hayley and Mark's vision for the ceremony. The initial email had said they wanted things pretty simple but not cheap. A country-style wedding with a killer dress, and the very best food. As Mark had said, "Let's burn our money on the stuff that matters."

Nicole guided them through the generalities—how many guests, would they write their own vows, how would security be handled, did they already have a photographer, who would do the service. At just the point Hayley and Mark were getting that dazed look—a signal to Nicole that they were both overwhelmed—it was time to go check out the dude ranch.

Sam took everyone in his roomy SUV, guys up front, and Nicole, Ginger and Hayley chatting happily about flowers in the back. The ranch was at the base of the foothills, about a forty-minute drive. With so much to talk about, the time passed quickly.

Hayley and Mark seemed to fall in love with the place as soon as they pulled off the main highway onto the gravel road with its overhead sign—*McGill Acres*. Horses grazed in the fields on both sides, and they could see the ranch house ahead. Everything about it felt serene, from the log cabin main lodge to the private cabins dotting the hillside to the immense barns. Henry and Sally McGill were already outside to greet them as they pulled into the circular drive, lined with bushes and flowers.

Nicole was impressed as soon as she met this warm couple. She could tell, just by shaking hands, that they had an easy-going energy about them that would permeate the entire wedding experience. They all started to move toward the main lodge. Watching the McGills talking to Hayley and Mark, who glancing lovingly at each other, Nicole suddenly felt like this was how she wished her relationship with Sam could have been when they got older.

The thought burst like a bubble out of the place she'd stuffed her love for Sam, and it shook her for a moment. As she refocused on the tasks at hand, she hoped—if Hayley and Mark decided to have the wedding here—that some of this couple's good energy might rub off on all of them.

The McGills led everyone first into the main lodge. Hayley and Mark both gasped at the sight of the enormous, round stone fireplace dominating the lounge area. People could sit comfortably on the stone bench all around it. Above the wide log mantle were several beautiful paintings of Wyoming landscapes. Leather couches and chairs in soft browns were arranged so guests could have a cozy chat. On the wide-plank wood floor were local Indian rugs in varied colors and sizes, this being Cheyenne territory after all. The walls and the ceiling were wood too, with wide log beams stretching across the expanse, holding chandeliers of tangled branches and light bulbs. Table lamps had wrought iron bases shaped like wagon wheels or cowboy boots, and all had lampshades with beaded fringe. A beautiful curved staircase led to a library nook with a balcony overlooking the bar area. The grand tour took them through the expansive kitchen, the guest rooms all done in colorful country quilts on fluffy beds, and through the wrap-around porch to the back lawn.

The view was truly breathtaking with lush green pastures nestled below the foothills and mountains rising to a big sky behind them. Nicole explained her vision of where the ceremony would take place. She pointed to an area near the dining hall where they could set up an arch made of graceful branches and cover it with flowers over the top and one side, asymmetrically, to serve as a backdrop for the couple. Chairs for the guests would go here, she gestured, and here. Hayley, with her uncle acting as her father who had died two years before, would be delivered by horse-drawn carriage to here. Nicole walked to the spot where Hayley would walk up the aisle. The couple beamed. Ginger gave Sam a look that said, yep, you nailed it. Sam smiled happily, then turned to wink at Nicole.

The reception would be at the dining hall with a huge outdoor patio area. Sally mentioned that others had put up strings of Christmas lights from beam to beam, crisscrossing the room. Hayley loved the idea. She wondered if they might also do the same outside, and Sally agreed. Nicole chimed in with her thoughts of antique oil lamps and candlesticks on tables with white linens. By this time, Mark and Hayley were beginning to really visualize how this could all go, and the excitement shone in their eyes.

Henry led them all next to one of the guest cabins and then to the honeymoon cabin. Everything was cozy, inviting, and still had all the modern conveniences.

"Mark, I don't want to leave," Hayley said gleefully. "This is so perfect. Even our friends used to five-star would be comfortable here."

They moved back to the main lodge to discuss possible dates, as this event would require reserving the entire ranch for a long weekend. Mark had a few more questions for Henry, mostly to do with security and privacy. When it seemed like the conversation was through, Sam and Nicole moved discreetly to the opposite end of the room to give the couple time to confer privately about their assessment of the venue.

After a few minutes of whispering amongst themselves, the couple and Ginger approached. "We really do like what we're seeing here," Hayley said. "I think you've captured just what we want. So you're hired." She smiled warmly and shook Nicole's hand.

Nicole beamed. "We're going to make this the wedding you've always dreamed of."

Hayley glanced at Mark, with a mixture of love and pain in her eyes.

Seeing the look, Nicole was reminded of their tumultuous beginning. They'd met at Cheyenne Frontier Days, where they'd had to share the stage for rehearsals. Both had been married at the time, and as it became obvious they were becoming an item, the tabloids ruthlessly printed every detail of their divorces and stolen time together. Nicole didn't normally read about such things, but while sitting in the dentist's office, a copy of *People* magazine had provided insight into her clients. And it made their upcoming wedding especially poignant for her.

Mark grabbed Hayley and smiled as he gave her a big happy hug.

Nicole informed the McGills and said she'd call soon to discuss contract details. Then they all piled in Sam's car to return to the airport as Hayley and Mark needed to get back to Nashville that night. They made it to the terminal with plenty of time to spare.

Nicole and Sam were elated, chatting excitedly about plans for the wedding, all the way back to her place.

chapter 20

When they walked in the door, Nicole took Sam by the hand and sat him down on the couch.

"So, Sam. Um, switching gears here. The rafting trip. Matt's coming. We have some…unfinished business, and he's coming here for that weekend." She tensed, waiting for the unpleasantness to come.

"Wow, that's just great, Nicole," he said sarcastically. Then he caught himself. The weekend was hardly going to go well if he kept that attitude. And as much as it hurt him to know there was another man in Nicole's life, he loved her too much to let anything come between them. In as normal a voice as he could muster, he said, "When will he get here?"

"I pick him up late Friday afternoon, and he goes home on Sunday morning."

He cringed, thinking of how much time Matt would have with

Nicole, have her in the way he wanted her so badly. He fervently wished he could trade in his heart, the one so irrevocably attached to Nicole, for a new one. Instead, the familiar resignation set in.

"That will make seven of us then. Has he ever been rafting before?"

"Nope. I think you said your friends haven't either, so we'll have three virgins." She instantly regretted her choice of words, saw Sam's jaw clench. *Oh, crap.*

He recovered though and said, "Yeah, could make for an even more interesting trip." He hopped off the couch, fiddled with his keys and tried to sound cheery. "Guess I'll be going then. I'll call you later with details about where to meet and such."

"Okay, Sam. Thanks." She turned back to her work, trying desperately to escape the tension of having hurt Sam. Yet again.

As he walked to his car, Sam could barely keep himself from crying.

I thought you said it was over with Matt. Why are you bringing him into our lives again? I've been waiting so long for you, so long. Nicole, are you ever coming back to me?

chapter 21

Matt's plane was a few minutes early—gotta love that jet stream—and Nicole hoped he wasn't yet out the pickup door. But as she pulled up, there he stood, in all his glorious cuteness. Her heart soared when he caught sight of her, and his mouth widened into that boyish grin she loved so much. *Damn dude, I have missed you.*

The minute she got out of the car, he was at her side, wrapping his arms around her. She melted into his body, felt his warmth, breathed in his totally Matt smell that so reminded her of ocean and sun. When they finally let go of each other, Matt kissed her long and hard. *Wow, why does this woman feel so much like home to me?*

The security guard broke them up with a "move along now, please." But he smiled in amusement as he walked past them.

Matt threw his bag in the car and climbed in the passenger seat.

"Thanks so much for taking the time to see me again," he said apologetically.

"Are you kidding? I'm absolutely delighted!" She gave him her warmest smile. As she drove, she could hardly take her eyes off him. She'd pictured him often in her mind since the camping trip and over time had decided she must have been exaggerating to herself about how good-looking he was. No one could be that gorgeous. *Oh, yes, they can be. And he most definitely is.* It wasn't just his features, or his blue eyes, or his tousled hair. His whole personality—sensitive, strong, sensual—shone through and put it all together in the complete package of Matt. Exquisite.

"So, are you hungry? Want to get something to eat before we head to my house?"

"Yeah, that would be much appreciated. I haven't eaten since…" He glanced at this watch. "Oh, damn, for a while now."

"Anything in particular sound good to you? Lots of choices on the way."

"Honestly, I'm not picky right now. Whatever's good."

"Hmm…Let's do the Chey Brewery then. They have plenty of variety, and they're not too noisy, so we can talk." She touched his leg, felt the thrill of the contact. "It's so good to see you again, Matt."

For a minute, he couldn't reply. The sudden intimate gesture made his blood flame, remembering their time together, very together, in her camper. Times he would always cherish. Wanted to repeat. Like right now. He forced himself back from the edge and croaked, "You too."

They arrived at the brewery quickly. Cheyenne wasn't exactly a big city. Not like San Diego, where you were almost never closer than thirty minutes to anywhere. When Nicole shut off the car, he started to reach for her, kiss her again, but stopped himself. He knew it wouldn't end with just a kiss. He wanted her too bad for just that. So he popped open his door and practically jumped out.

Nicole was a bit shocked, watching him pull away. *Did I read something wrong? Thought we'd connected before*...She got out and was locking the door when Matt came up and took her hand. *Oh, okay.* Together they walked into the restaurant.

The atmosphere was always friendly in Chey Brewery. Owned by a family who'd moved from a small Colorado town, not unlike Cheyenne, western memorabilia was everywhere. If they ever sold it all to an antique dealer they could make a fortune. The 1840s bar alone, with its rich mahogany top, hand-carved base and mirrored wall unit that matched, was a sight.

Matt and Nicole were seated by the hostess almost immediately. The usual Friday night crowd hadn't yet arrived. With menus in their hands, ignored menus, they sat staring at each other for a minute, drinking each other in.

The waiter who came over was built and cute, and it was obvious his method of working a table was to be just on the edge of flirty with the women because he focused his attention primarily on Nicole.

He winked at her, and said, "So sweetheart. What would you like to drink?"

Nicole glared at him. *Yeah, honey, you're all right. But have you seen the guy sitting across from me? Get a clue—he's much hotter than you could ever be. Might want to back off a bit.*

The waiter took their drink orders and left.

"I have a little surprise for you," she said to Matt.

He raised his eyebrow. "And it is..."

"We're going rafting tomorrow. My friend Sam has some

buddies from college coming into town, and that's the main thing they want to do. My sister and her husband are going too. Ooh, are you up for meeting my family?"

Why hadn't this occurred to her before, that he might be uncomfortable meeting her family and friends. They'd been in such a bubble while camping, almost like they weren't really in each other's real lives. This would be a whole new level for them.

"Depends on how you're going to introduce me. As long as I'm just a friend…I especially don't want to tread on Sam's toes. I remember you said he's pretty attached to you."

"Actually, I've already told him a lot about you." Matt blanched, so she hastily added, "Oh, not the really personal stuff. I would never. I mean that we spent time together, that's all."

"How did he take it? I mean, this guy seriously cares about you, doesn't he? If I were in his shoes, what happened with us in your camper would cut me to the core."

God, how many times had she hurt Sam this way? She always told him about the guys she spent time with, as he used to tell her about his women when he'd dated. He'd said he wanted to know, insisted on the details. But every time the intense pain in his eyes was unmistakable, and she'd had to steel herself to get the words out. Hearing Matt be so sensitive to Sam's feelings just emphasized how torturous her so-called friendship with Sam had been for him.

"He took it like he always does—like a trooper. I feel like a real shit now. Sam's always so sweet to me." She dropped her head, embarrassed, and sighed heavily.

"Nicole, that wasn't my intention at all. Tell me more about this rafting thing we're doing."

She brightened but resolved to revisit her treatment of Sam, in the future.

"Well, we're to meet the others at nine, and then we'll consolidate cars to get up the hill. Sam picked an easy section of the river cause his friends haven't done this before. I'm guessing you haven't either?"

"No, and it sounds like a kick, so this is great."

"After, we can do a late lunch. Maybe do a short hike if you want, or I can give you a tour of Cheyenne?"

"Fun day. I do want you to myself in the evening though. Is that okay?"

"Absolutely." She gave him a wink.

The waiter came back and served their drinks with an unnecessary flourish, holding them high above his head then swooping them in for a landing on the table. This kid was starting to get on Nicole's nerves. Matt seemed to be watching her reaction to him and enjoying it though, so she just laughed.

"What will you be having tonight?" the waiter said, leaning in rather too closely toward her.

"I think I'll have this gin and tonic, and then Matt here, and then the salmon with lemon butter," she said sweetly. Both men blushed. The waiter quickly turned to get Matt's order.

"I'll have the tenderloin medallions and sautéed mushrooms, medium."

"Very good." The waiter turned on his heel and practically sprinted away. Matt burst out laughing.

"That was pretty good! Now how would you like me—rare? Medium well?"

"Did you say *bare*?" She batted her eyes at him. "That sounds really good to me."

That one little word, in a flash, brought back all the intimate times they'd had, and Matt's blood surged. He sucked in his breath.

"Oh, you are a wild one, aren't you?"

"And you are hotter than molten lava, Matt. I'd been trying to put you out of my mind, thought we were past, but now…"

The heat between them was rising fast. Her eyes blazed, and he was beginning to lose that self-control he'd exercised earlier in the car. With the little he had left he said, "We're never going to make it through this meal at this rate, Nicole. Let's finish these drinks and cool down some."

She gave him her most pathetic pout but said, "Agreed. Do you want to start talking about something more serious, like your dreams?"

"Whoa, talk about a downshift." His eyes went from electricity-charged to dead-serious in a heartbeat. "But, yes, if that's okay with you."

"So, tell me what's still bothering you." She took a long swig of her gin and tonic and settled in.

"Look, I hear you say that I have to accept that part of myself. But I have no idea how to see what that piece can do, like in my dreams, and say to it 'you're okay' when everything I've ever been taught says *wrong*. There's just too much distance between those two."

"Well, let's backtrack a bit. What do you think I mean when I say the word accept? Are you thinking I mean you have to think it's good, that you have to like it? Because that's not at all what I mean by accept."

He cocked his head to one side, and his face lightened a little.

She continued. "When I told you I had accepted that part of me that could hurt a child, did you think that meant I thought it was good or that I liked it? Hell no, says the human me. Where I've come to with that piece is this: it's there, I don't know why—don't have the infinite wisdom to understand why—but something that knows much more than I do put it there, and so I will not fight it."

"Fight—that's a good word to use. Because that's really what I do, is fight it, resist it. If I don't, won't I wind up doing something awful?"

"No, I don't think so. That piece of me made itself known, and it was present for a while in my life, in my thoughts. But it never pushed for expression in the physical world. It just sat in the background, so to speak. Could it come forward at some point? Sure, that's not impossible. But I don't think it will. It hasn't even been in my awareness for years, until we talked."

"Do you think that could happen for me?"

"Yes. But you have to accept, let it be there without the resistance. Have you ever heard the expression 'what you resist persists'?"

"No, I haven't. Is that why the dreams keep coming back?"

"Quite likely. That piece, for whatever reason, wants recognition and acceptance. Again, for you, I do not believe that means it wants to express in 'real life.' For you, expression in dream form seems to be enough to satisfy it. But clearly it wants to be seen, wants you to acknowledge that it's in your cast of characters, so to speak. It doesn't want to be ignored and pushed away." She paused, thought for a bit.

"I have an idea. Close your eyes."

Matt hesitated, then did as she asked.

"Now, just relax a minute. Let your mind go blank. Now see a stage. At first, it's empty, no one there. Can you see it?"

Matt nodded, eyes still closed.

"Now bring in that part of you and watch him as he takes the woman from behind and snaps her neck. Try, really try, not to get emotionally caught up in the image, just let it be what it is with no judgment. Can you do that?"

Matt's face was tight, and his hands started to curl up into fists. Clearly, he was resisting the experience. But he held to it, and finally his hands uncurled, his face relaxed. When he opened his eyes, they were filled with awe.

"Man, that works, it really works! At first it was awful, but then I started to see it as something separate from me. Well, not completely separate—it is my dream. But separate like it's not *all* of me, like there's another part of me that can just watch it but not *be* it. Does that make any sense?"

"Oh, definitely. What you just went into is called the witness state, where you can watch something yet not be attached to it, not feel identified with it. It's pretty powerful, isn't it?"

Matt nodded furiously as the waiter brought their food. Even through questions about whether he wanted ketchup or hot sauce, or another drink, his eyes shone with the new realization.

"So is that kind of what you mean by accepting it? To just see it and let it be there without doing anything else about it?"

"Yep, that's about it." She looked at their plates. "Want to concentrate on eating for a bit while you hold that experience?"

Matt took a big bite of his steak and grinned. They ate in silence for a while. Nicole left him to his own thoughts, knowing it had been a radical shift for him. His eyes told her he was continuing to work with what she'd called the witness state. He couldn't believe such a simple exercise could turn things around so quickly, but there it was. Hopefully, he could hold onto it.

After a few minutes, he said, "I feel like something really heavy in me has just dropped away. Looking at that stage inside made me see just how small that part is in my life, how much more there is of me. I didn't see them, but there must be so many more characters who could be on my stage, way more than just that one." He paused, reflecting. "In fact, it felt like there were tons of them on the side, just watching that part, not even really connected to him."

"Oh yeah, Matt. Once you get started looking at the internal stage, it's astounding how many different pieces you can see. And when you start feeling how they all interact, which ones come forward and when, which ones dominate others, how many are still stuck in child states of mind—well, it certainly blows me away."

"Jeez. How do you even get a handle on it all?"

She laughed. "I doubt there's a human being on this planet who can. Best we can do is deal with what comes up for us."

They'd finished their entrees and sat looking at each other, both thinking how lucky they were to have that extraordinary person across the table in their lives. When the waiter came, timidly, to ask about dessert, they declined. He cleared their dishes and left to get the check.

"Okay, I think it's starting to sink in." The look on Matt's face turned to an earnest longing. "I want you, Nicole, bad."

Instantly her eyes went liquid as desire consumed her. Breathlessly she whispered, "Me too."

They paid the check as quickly as they could. Even the waiter could tell it was important he get them out of there fast, otherwise he was likely to have to explain to his boss why the morning headlines would read "Mating Ritual in Local Bar Has Patrons Gawking."

Matt tried to keep his hands off Nicole while she drove them back to her place, but he wasn't very successful. He caressed her cheek, kissed her bare shoulder, ran his hand up her thigh until she pleaded with him to stop. “Aargh, you drive me crazy! It’s not fair when I can’t touch you back.”

His grin almost tipped her over the edge.

“If you don’t cut that out, I’m going to pull over right here on Maple Street, screw your brains out, and we’ll both spend the night in jail for indecent exposure.”

Matt relented. “You have a point. How much longer?”

“We’re almost there, thank god.”

Nicole had already turned off the engine as they pulled into the drive then parked. Laughing, they raced to see who could get into the house first. They peeled their clothes off in record time, eyes fixed on each other. Matt was already at “half-mast” and Nicole marveled at his lean, tight body. He sucked in his breath, seeing her soft, full curves again and pulled her to him in a dancing pose. Round and round they twirled, bodies entwined, skin electrified by the touch of skin.

Kisses and caresses quickly grew more passionate, and she feared they would both crash to the floor if she didn’t get them to bed, soon. She pulled away, took hold of his hand and led him to her bedroom.

Standing by the edge of the bed, Matt’s mouth on hers was warm and insistent. She could feel the fever overtaking her. She pulled him onto the bed, onto her. Filled with an almost unbearable wanting, she eased him into her. He moaned deeply and with a seductive and relentless rhythm brought them both to a crescendo of pleasure. They came together, in bliss.

chapter 22

Waking up together with the morning's sunshine streaming through the window brought back memories of their time in the camper's bed, happy sexy times, and they were soon tangled up again. This left them without enough time to go out for breakfast, so they quickly got dressed and threw together a couple of ham and cheese omelets. When they settled down to eat, Nicole prodded Matt.

"Okay, give it up. How are things going with Amanda?"

His face fell.

"Oh crap, Nicole. I haven't called her yet. Can't tell you how many times I picked up the phone, but as soon as I pulled up her number, I just couldn't do it. I kept thinking about how I would explain things to her, and I knew I didn't have the words. I barely understand it. That's why I called you, wanted to be with you again. There's something about being with you that makes me *feel* what you're telling me."

"That's called induction, Matt. The energetics of what I know are passed to you, even apart from the spoken words."

"Whatever you call it, it works."

"You know you've never really told me much about her. How did you two meet?"

"Freshman year of college. I walked into my English lit class, and there she was, chatting it up with a friend. Amanda was the most beautiful girl I'd ever seen. I never believed in that stuff before, but it really was love at first sight. She didn't see me then, and I spent two weeks trying to work it so I'd wind up sitting next to her in that class. No luck. Finally, I just waited outside till she and her friends came, and kind of ambushed her. Most bungled invitation to get coffee ever. And she said yes!" His face still registered surprise at the thought.

"Of course she did, Matt. Who wouldn't?"

"It was kind of a whirlwind after that. We just *fit*. We spent every minute we could together. She'd wanted to be a veterinarian since she was a kid, so she was pretty serious about school, which was a good thing. Otherwise, we'd never have studied."

Nicole smiled.

"I was pretty lost back then, had no idea what I wanted to do with my life, and she kept me on track with classes. Second semester a friend of hers dropped out, so we took over her apartment and got married end of June. On the beach." His face drifted away at the memory, happy at first, then wistful.

"Wow, I bet that was gorgeous. I've always thought it would be amazing to do a wedding on the beach—with the rhythmic waves of the ocean, and soft breezes, and drinks with little umbrellas in them."

He chuckled.

"It was great. My dad loved Amanda. In fact, I think they still talk once in a while. And her parents loved me, until after the end of junior year I decided I needed something different than college. That's when the urge to join the Army hit me. No one could understand why because it looked from the outside like I had it all laid out for me. You know: college, marriage, working for my dad's business, some kids. Complete with dogs since Amanda would be a vet. She didn't understand either, but she supported me in the decision. Oh, Nicole, she was so supportive..."

Sadness settled over him again, and it was a minute before he could go on.

"It was really hard to leave her and go to basic training. Then I got stationed not too far away for a while, and we braved through it, seeing each other when we could. Every time we got together, we would concentrate on making our plans for the future—where we'd live, what kind of house we wanted, how many kids. I guess it shouldn't have been, but it was a real shock when I got the orders I was being sent to Iraq. She cried so hard. When I left, she tried to keep the fear off her face, but after I walked away, I turned back, and she was sobbing, those ones that shake your whole body. Broke my heart." His shoulders sagged, and a gloom swept over his face as he remembered that day.

"Oh, Matt." She reached out and gently touched his shoulder.

"Anyway, you kind of know what happened after that. Iraq, coming home and not being able to talk to her, or make love to her. When she finally gave up on me and told me she wanted a divorce, it about killed me. But I didn't fight it. She deserved better than I could give. Then." He looked at Nicole with the deepest gratitude in his misting eyes. "Now, I feel like I might have a chance to get her back. Thanks to you." He took her hand and raised it to his lips.

“Matt there’s nothing in the world I want more than for you to have that chance.” She gently scolded him, “But you have to call her.”

“Yeah, I know. I’ll do it. I will.”

Nicole glanced at the clock and realized how late it was getting. Sam was going to be upset if they held up the rafting trip. She got Matt to rinse off the dishes—they could wash them later—while she put away the food. Then they scrambled out the door.

chapter 23

Nicole and Matt pulled into her sister's drive just in time to see Sam and his friends walking in the front door.

"Whoa, nice house," Matt said.

"Isn't it?" Nicole replied. "Wait till you see inside."

Jen and Nick had managed to build their dream house, not a large one, but filled with all the features that really mattered to them. Nick was one of Cheyenne's finest architects. Most of the mega-mansions in the area were done by him now. He'd had a real blast designing their own home. The front door was hand carved by a local artist, the chandelier over the dining table—also by a local artist—was an intricate design of metal and crystals of all cuts and sizes. Most of the family's living happened in the great room, full of warm colors, soft pillows, simple furniture and a huge stone fireplace at one end. The space flowed naturally into the kitchen with its intimate eating nook and white and glass door cabinets. It was all built to be lived in, spacious and cozy all at the same time.

"Hey, you're all here, on time!" Jen yelled.

"We are. I'd like you to meet my friends John and Paul." Sam made a sweeping gesture with his hands as though he were selling blenders on a home shopping show.

"You guys didn't bring George and Ringo with you?" Nicole kidded. "Great to meet you. And I'd like you all to meet Matt," she said with the same flourish Sam had used.

As everyone said hi, Matt noticed Sam stared at him a lot more intensely than was usual for a first meeting. *I think I'm going to have to be pretty careful around him.*

Everyone else introduced themselves to the newcomers, and they worked out which cars they would ride in. Nick and Sam were driving, so Sam's friends would go with him while the other three would ride with Nick. Matt just happened to be looking at Sam when all this was being decided. Obviously, Sam didn't like it that Nicole wouldn't be in his car.

The babysitter was already in back playing with the kids, so as soon as Jen popped her head out to shout goodbye to them, they all loaded up and headed out.

On the drive out of the city, it became obvious that Jen, Nick and Matt were going to get along just fine. They chatted easily about where everyone grew up, where they'd lived—all the usual first meeting topics. Then Matt discovered Nick was an architect, and Nick learned of Matt's interest in history, and architectural history dominated the conversation the rest of the way to the rafting office.

As they got out of the car, Jen caught Nicole's eye. She pursed her lips and cocked her head in a "yeah sis, Matt be all right" nod.

Nicole flushed, and grinned. No matter how old she got, her older sister's approval would always mean something to her.

They'd arrived at the rafting company with a few minutes to spare. Walking to the office, Matt instinctively put his arm around Nicole and gave her a hug, until he saw the intense expression on Sam's face. *Oh yeah, got to keep it cool around him.*

They filled out all the paperwork, release forms, then were led to another room to be fitted for life jackets. There was another group of six to go down the river at the same time, in another raft. Once they were all dressed up like orange pumpkins, their guide introduced himself.

"Hi, I'm Jimmy, and I'll be taking this first group here," he said, pointing to the seven of them.

"So a few safety rules. Don't stand up in the rafts, row only when I tell you to, and don't lean over the side. If you do fall in, do not try to stand up—you can get your foot caught in the rocks, which is a bad thing. If you can't grab the raft and the current takes you, be sure to float feet first until you can either get back in the raft or get to the riverbank." He straightened himself up tall and crossed his arms over his chest. In his deepest stern voice, he said, "And you must obey me, your master, at all times."

Everyone chuckled, and he spelled out some more rules of the river. When he finished, and the rafts were loaded on the trailer, they climbed into the bus for the trip to the river landing point. Matt intentionally struck up a conversation with Nick again, so he could sit with him on the bus, leaving the seat next to Nicole open. Jen took it quickly. She wanted a little sis-to-sis time. Sam tried to hide it, but his look of relief was not to be missed by anyone who knew the situation.

There were other rafts at the landing point when they arrived, so they had to wait their turn before putting in. Once in the water, the fun began. Matt couldn't believe how similar rafting was to surfing, just a larger "vehicle" really. It wasn't long before he was anticipating what Jimmy would tell them to do as they approached a boulder or a rapid, and he essentially became the guide's right-hand man. With Nicole beside him, this wonderfully important woman in his life, he felt the happiest he'd felt in a very long time.

Nicole was happy too. All her favorite people were here, together, sharing an adventure. Even Sam was now enjoying himself, laughing and tossing around bad jokes with John and Paul. She knew he really loved the river, almost as much as she did. He was seated in front of her, and as she watched his body move to maneuver the raft through the current, she felt how much she loved her friend—for the flash of an instant, even remembered what it felt like to run her hands over his shoulder, his back, his stomach and down. She blushed, disconcerted by the thought. *Way too much "man" in this boat, making me go all crazy,* she decided.

When they reached a calmer section of the river, Jimmy announced it was time for a swim. One by one, they all jumped off the raft into the cool water. John, ever the troublemaker, splashed Paul in the face, and it quickly turned into a massive free-for-all water fight. Nicole and Jen tried as best as they could to stay out of the way. This was a pure testosterone event, confirming Nicole's earlier thoughts.

It became obvious to the women that frustrations were being vented. In a short time, the general fighting had been reduced to

John versus Paul, and Sam with Matt. Nick joined in from time to time but was clearly an extra in this mix. Nicole was especially interested in the dynamic unfolding with the two men in her life. Sam was aggressively going after Matt, who responded in kind at first. Then, realizing all this was really about Sam's trying to establish territorial rights over Nicole, he backed off and returned Sam's hard splashes with much gentler ones. Finally, Sam relented as he understood that Matt was not going to fight him.

Jen and Nicole exchanged meaningful glances, no words necessary.

"Okay, boys and girls. Time to head on down the river," Jimmy said.

The guys got back to the raft first as Nicole and Jen had moved further away to avoid the fighting. Nick pulled Jen up and gave her a loving squeeze.

Nicole splashed her way back to the raft and looked up to see two hands reaching out to help her up—one Sam's and one Matt's. In the flash of an instant, she recognized the choice she had, and extended her hand to Sam.

Matt quickly withdrew. The look on Sam's face clearly expressed he was in full "taking care of my woman" mode. Matt watched as Sam pulled her in and held her just a little closer and longer than necessary to make sure she was steady. *I wonder if she realizes how significant that was, choosing Sam's hand. I could see it in her eyes—she loves him. Why is she holding back? He obviously loves her too. I don't get it.*

They were all sad when the landing came into view, and they knew the journey was over. When they pulled up to the river's edge, Nicole leaped out of the raft before either Sam or Matt could "help" her. She'd had enough of the competitive nonsense between these two. Neither seemed to notice though, so she took her seat next to Jen on the ride back to the office and decided to let it all go.

chapter 24

Nick announced he was hungry for pizza and asked if that would be okay with everyone. He got a resounding *yes* as a response. So they started down the hill to Pete's.

Walking into the joint, the first thing Matt's eyes were drawn to was the enormous brick oven. Some talented bricklayer had made it his masterpiece; its picture had been on the cover of *Restaurateur* magazine several years ago. Used brick, set on slanted curves, gave the feeling the oven was undulating from top to bottom. Matt had never seen anything like it.

The hostess sat their party at a table next to a window, which overlooked the river they'd just rafted. Matt made a point of sitting next to Nick, leaving the seat by Nicole for Sam. She was touched by Matt's sensitivity and, when Sam's head was turned so he couldn't see, blew him a kiss. Matt smiled and winked.

The lunch buffet was still on for another half hour, plenty of time to get their fill. Pete's always had a dozen pies out, so there'd be something for everyone, except thin crust. Pete's was thick whole wheat. They set out honey to put on the edges once the center was eaten. This was not a place to diet.

After the waiter had taken their drink orders—beers all around—they filed to the buffet table and loaded up. By the time they'd started eating, Paul was ribbing Sam about the dunking he'd gotten.

"Dude, I'm still wet, you know. I squish when I sit."

Sam grinned from ear to ear. "Just consider it payback for the time you puked all over me at that party junior year. Do you even remember that? At least the water in your pants doesn't smell to high heaven." He puckered up his face. "Or does it?"

Nicole broke in. "You're lucky he didn't pull a kung fu move on you. Squishing would have been the least of your problems."

The tone of sincere admiration in her voice, and the look of affection on her face made both Matt and Jen stare at her. Sam was too caught up in his discomfort around Matt's presence to notice.

"Still foul!" Paul called out. "Seriously though, that rafting is a kick. I want to go again next time we're out here."

"You got it," Sam said, then turned to John. "Did you like it?"

John had just put half a slice of pizza in his mouth so could only nod his assent.

Matt agreed. "I'd go again this afternoon if Nicole and I didn't have other things to do." *Oh, shit. Open mouth, insert foot.* Quickly he added, "She's going to show me around Cheyenne."

Sam's mouth was set in a grim line, but he didn't say anything. Nicole picked up the thread.

"I thought maybe I would show him the Cheyenne Frontier Days complex."

"Yes, and don't forget the railroad museum," added Jen.

She could see the tension between Sam and Matt, and the almost panicked look on Nicole's face. Trying to make things lighter she said, "Hey, has anyone seen that movie, *Up in the Air*? I know it's not exactly new, but Nick and I just saw it the other night, and it has the coolest beginning. You know before the movie even starts. Some woman is singing 'This Land Is Our Land' while you see all these pictures of America from the air—cities and towns and crop circles and rivers. Whoever did that really put it together like a mosaic, and it gives you such a sense of how expansive and varied this country is."

"Oh, I remember that one, and what you're talking about," Matt said. "That was extraordinary."

"Okay, favorite quotes from a movie," Nick prompted.

John immediately blurted out, "*Ferris Bueller's Day Off*, at the very end of the movie, after the credits, when he comes out in his pajamas. 'Are you all still here? Go home.' Classic."

"*Galaxy Quest*," Jen said, "when Tim Allen and Sigourney Weaver are having to go through that chomper tunnel, which doesn't seem to have any real purpose. She asks him why it's there, and he says it's there because the original show had it. And she says, 'well this scene was badly written.' I could say that about a number of 'scenes' in my life!"

Sam nodded enthusiastically, then added "In *An Ideal Husband*, when Minnie Driver is telling Rupert Jones 'To look at a thing is not the same as seeing a thing. To really see a thing, one has to see its beauty.' So true."

"Hmm, I like that one," Matt said thoughtfully. "I always thought it was funny, in *Romancing the Stone*, when Mike Douglas and Kathleen Turner come up to the drug runner's house, and he says 'write us out of this one, Joan Wilder,' and it turns out the drug lord loves her books, gives them anything they want. Funny how this unassuming author turns the tide for them."

Nicole reflected for a moment. "Power is an interesting, and tricky, thing. I love that scene in *Big Miracle,* where they're debating about asking the Russians for help saving three whales trapped by the ice cause they're the only ones with an icebreaker close by. At the table is the CEO of a big oil company with tons of money, a military guy with all that might behind him, and a dedicated lady who works for an underfunded environmental group. She calmly says something like—if you don't let the Russians help, then I'm going to tell the world President Reagan killed those whales. Suddenly all the money and military strength are nothing. Just a few words have brought them to their knees. It makes you realize how quickly it can all flip. Like how a simple act of love can overcome longtime hatred."

"Ah, yes, love. There's nothing like a good love story," Sam said bitterly.

"Then again, sometimes you need a shot of adrenaline," Paul chimed in, not aware of the tension in his friend. "Anyone remember *True Lies*, with Arnold and Jamie Lee Curtis? That part when he's in the Harrier? And he's shooting up the terrorists in the office building? Blasting out all those windows? Man, when I'm seriously pissed about something, I love to watch that scene."

"Sam, you should take this guy shooting." Nicole turned to Paul. "Have you ever shot a pistol?"

"No, my family was pretty much anti-gun."

"Oh, dude, you'd love it. Even when you're just shooting a paper target, the power of that gun going off can really release the energy."

"I'd like to try too," John said. "Any chance we three could do that tomorrow, before we go back?"

"Sure," Sam agreed. "Maybe in the morning before the crowds come in. Think you can get your butts out of bed early?"

"Yeah, yeah."

All the guys got up to hit the buffet again, leaving Nicole and Jen to talk.

"I really like Matt," Jen said. "He seems really sweet, and he's trying so hard to be nice to Sam. Who's being kind of a dick actually."

"Yeah, but we both know why. God, Jen, maybe I shouldn't have brought Matt today. I just wanted you to get a chance to meet him."

"Well, I'm glad you did." She raised her eyebrows. "Pretty interesting, him showing up here again. Think there might be a future for you two?"

Nicole rested her chin on her hand and looked thoughtfully at her sister. "Well, I don't see how. We live half a country apart, and that's not the greatest distance. Matt's still in love with Amanda, his wife, well, ex. And if I'm honest with myself, I never did have the sense that we would wind up together, long term. There's no denying we have an intense connection, deeper than anything I've had except for Sam. But it doesn't feel like love. It's more like we've been put in each other's lives to learn something…"

"Well, whatever you want to call it, being around him sure lights you up. It's great to see."

Nicole smiled. "Oh, yes, indeed." Her face grew somber. "I do wonder though how it will affect things with Sam."

"You know Sam will get over this. He always does when you

have another guy. And isn't Matt leaving tomorrow? You can make it up to Sam then."

Nicole let out an anguished sigh. *Is it because I've hurt Sam again? Or because Matt's leaving? Crap—probably both.* "Yeah, guess so."

When they got back to Nick and Jen's, and they'd all piled out of their cars, Jen invited everyone in for a drink.

"Actually, I think we're just going to head out," Nicole said. "But thanks."

She hugged her sister, then Nick, and turned to hug Sam. His face was tight, and he stood stiff as she wrapped her arms around him. His head was filled with unwelcome thoughts of what would surely happen between Nicole and Matt in the hours before Matt left. Nicole felt his pain, but there was nothing she could do for him.

She and Matt finished their goodbyes to the others, and left quickly.

chapter 25

As they drove away, Matt said, "Man, that guy is really stuck on you, Nicole."

She grimaced, and her hands were tense on the wheel. "I know, Matt. Could we just not talk about this please? It's not something I can fix right now."

Matt put his hand on her arm, gave it a gentle squeeze. He leaned over and kissed her cheek.

"Show me your town, darlin,'" he said in his best country drawl, still not right, but so cute. It made Nicole smile, and she relaxed into the afternoon.

As they came into Cheyenne from the north, Nicole drove him first to the complex of Cheyenne Frontier Days. It brought back memories of Sam, normally cherished memories, but today she had to push them aside. She needed to not think about that sensual smile the first time she saw him, his kiss in the hallway, his all-encompassing body-to-body hugs. Not today.

"So Matt, have you ever been to a rodeo?"

"No, I haven't. I've seen them in movies, of course, but never live."

"Dude, you really have to come back sometime and experience it for real. The excitement is off the charts. And you've already got the hat for it." Her heart skipped, remembering how hot he'd looked that day at Jack's, buying his cowboy gear.

He grinned. "I do, indeed. What's your favorite part of the rodeo?"

"Honestly, I love the barrel racing. I mean the bull riding and the bronc riding are cool too, but I'm always worried someone is going to get hurt. They really do sometimes. And watching those horses pirouetting around the barrels—they turn on a dime. It's amazing to see."

"Sounds great. I guess all the events are based on skills they must have needed to deal with herds of cattle and so forth." Matt's love of history was kicking in. "I bet the long cattle drives were quite the challenge."

"Yeah, you know there are still a few dude ranches around here that will give you that experience, in miniature, of course. You can spend a week driving cattle from one feedlot to another. Might be kind of fun for you to do some time, now that you can ride a horse."

"Oh, sure, I wouldn't be able to walk for months if I did that." Matt laughed.

They drove into the center of town then, to the depot square, and Nicole told him about the gunslinger routines some of the locals put on for tourists during the busy summer. Matt was interested, and asked questions from time to time, but he also seemed to be occupied with something churning in his mind. She wished he would say what was going on.

The Cheyenne Depot Railroad Museum pulled him out of his reverie. Nicole had never seen anyone read every single plaque for every single exhibit before. When he finally reached the end, he suggested they find someplace to get a coffee and talk a bit. They decided to drive to the little local coffee house close to Nicole's home. Matt seemed distant as they stood in line for their drinks, and Nicole was beginning to feel uneasy. When they sat down, she decided to just ask.

"So Matt, it feels like you've got something on your mind. What's going on?"

"Well, yes. And I'm not sure how to bring this up. When we were camping…how could you be so sure I wouldn't hurt you, after all the things I told you?"

"Matt, I didn't *know*. I just felt like you wouldn't. It's all about energy. Do you know what I mean by that?" He shook his head. "Do you ever walk up to someone and just have a feeling about them? Like an almost full-body response of, 'ooh I need to steer clear of this one, he doesn't feel trustworthy'?"

"Oh, yeah. I do. One of my professors once. He just felt squirmy to me, like he would wiggle out from under me if I let him. Turned out, he was really like that too. He got caught selling grades to students. Is that what feeling energy is like?"

"Basically, yes. Sometimes your body reads the energy of another person better than your mind can. What you see in another person can be deceiving—nice clothes, pleasant face and so on. Looks can hide a very ugly soul. If you can 'feel into' someone, your body can often tell you when you need to watch out."

"Oh, and is that what you did with me?"

"Yes. When I tuned in to you, nothing felt off. You felt authentic, respectful, good. So when you told me all that stuff, it was almost a disconnect for me. Like that stuff is not really this person, it's not who he is at a soulic level. I'm okay with him."

"Wow. Well, I can't begin to tell you how much that meant to me. To have you see me, even the very worst parts of me, and still accept me, allow me to be with you..." His eyes reddened, and Nicole touched his arm gently.

"Matt, do you remember what I said to you the first time we made love?"

He looked at her questioningly, trying to bring it back.

"I said you're very precious."

The mist in his eyes turned to tears.

"And I meant it. I wish you could see yourself the way I see you, then you'd understand."

"But what if Amanda can't see me that way?" he blurted. "What if Amanda can't feel energy like you do, and she can only hear the awful things and think that's all of me?" His eyes pleaded with Nicole for an answer, begged for some assurance that he wasn't going to lose the woman he loved so much.

Her look of tender concern made his heart sink. "Matt, I know you want me to tell you that everything is going to be okay. But I can't do that. Amanda will have to deal with all this in the only way she can, and neither of us knows how that will be. And honestly, it's not your job to make her see things your way or make her love you again. Your only job will be to present yourself as truthfully and openly as you can. You'll have to be very vulnerable, which is hard. I know. Just remember that you were able to do that with me. You love her, so I know you can be open to her."

"Oh, Nicole. Somehow you always have exactly the right

thing to say to me, exactly what I need to hear. I just hope I can remember this conversation when I talk to Amanda. I'm so afraid of her reaction."

"That fear will get transmitted to her, you know," she said, her tone growing serious. "You don't want to be in that frame of mind when you approach her. You need to find a way to be calm, so she'll be able to feel who you really are, not the fear. Do you remember how you felt when you saw that dream part of you on the stage, and then you were able to see it as something separate from you? Bring that back, before you talk to her."

"Oh yeah. That was so incredible. You're right. If I can feel like that, I might be able to pull this off." His face brightened. "Thank you, Nicole." He kissed her hand, then smiled.

Oh, he's back, Nicole thought gratefully. And yet, she was starting to feel a separation...

"So what's the next bit of Cheyenne history you're going to show me?" he asked excitedly.

"Well, how about the Old West Museum?"

"Sounds wonderful," he said as he got up. "You ready?"

chapter 26

They landed at the Vault for dinner, which was exactly the setting of this unusual restaurant. In the basement of an old bank building, much of the seating was in the vault, behind one of those massive bolted doors. It made for a dark but intimate space, where you could have a private conversation. It was one of Nicole's favorite places, although a bit pricey.

After ordering drinks, Nicole and Matt chatted happily about the rafting trip, the others Matt had met and Cheyenne.

"I really like your sister, and Nick. And actually Sam too. You've got some good people in your life, Nicole."

"I know. I'm so grateful. Not everybody has family and friends who are so great. I'm really glad you liked them. It means a lot to me. You mean a lot to me."

Her words went straight to his heart, leaving Matt uncertain what to say next. Nicole meant a lot to him too, but he wasn't sure he could put words to how he felt yet. Luckily, the waitress returned with their meals, and eating became their focus.

After a few minutes, Matt struck up conversation again.

"Okay, now it's my turn." Matt had such a weighty, almost stern, expression that Nicole stopped with a bite of salmon and lettuce halfway to her mouth. Nervously, she put her fork down, almost afraid to hear what he was going to say. *Have I done something wrong, pissed him off?*

"Nicole. You belong with Sam. Like really. You need to let that man in."

Her sigh of relief was cut short when she saw how deadly serious he was. His tone had made the words more like a command than a suggestion, and deep down, she felt the truth of them.

"Crap, Matt, I know it." Her shoulders sagged.

"Honestly, I have no idea why you haven't grabbed onto him with both hands. He's so fun to be with. He loves you with all of his heart. That's insanely obvious. He'd do anything for you. And has, if I get your history right. He's so loyal, like a dog who loves his master no matter what. I don't get why you keep shutting him out."

Criminy Matt, neither do I. I've been over this a million times in my head...

"Fear. Nothing fancy, just plain old fear."

"Oh, really. That sounds a bit funny coming from you, who expect me to get past mine, accept my most horrible aspects, and even have the courage to tell Amanda." A hint, well more than just a hint, of anger flashed across his face. She cringed.

"Matt, I told you about Jason, what my marriage was like..."

"Yeah, well, that was a long time ago, right? And Sam is not Jason, right? Don't you think it might be time to get over that shit?"

The force with which he spit out the words shocked her. Suddenly, she felt backed in a corner. It didn't make sense. She wasn't being threatened, not really. But even though her head knew that, something in her, on the deep emotional level, most definitely did not. She shrank back in her chair, and her frightened look made Matt shudder.

"Oh, Nicole, I'm sorry. I wasn't trying to upset you. You know how much I care about you." He looked so desperate, her feelings of sympathy softened her reaction to his blast.

"Matt, I do know. I'm sorry too. I feel like a complete hypocrite. And honestly, I don't know why I'm so afraid. I can't even begin to tell you how many times I've tried to work through this. Remember I told you that everyone has pieces of themselves still stuck in child mode?"

Matt nodded.

"I know that it's a child in me that carries the fear because it grips me so hard. The piece doesn't have any resources to deal with it, just like say a three-year-old wouldn't be able to. Understand?"

"Not sure..."

"Well, imagine I have a three-year-old inside who's running the whole show, like she's the only one on stage, with no help. That piece can't handle much, certainly not something as complicated as a grown-up relationship. So she panics."

"Oh, yeah, I see. Well, what's she so panicked about?"

"I don't know. She won't tell me. I've asked her over and over, and I get nothing. It's like whenever I get close, she just starts crying."

Her helpless look touched Matt to the core. She'd always been the strong one in their friendship, and now here she was, cowering with her own problems. An inspiration struck. He cocked his head to the side and raised an eyebrow.

"Want to try something?"

"Ohh kay..."

With a tender and serious expression, he said, "Nicole, will you marry me?"

In an instant, all the blood drained from her face, and Matt feared she might fall to the floor. Quickly he said, "Now, what was the very first thing you felt when I said that?"

"That I wouldn't be enough for you to want to stay with me." Her eyes widened as the realization fully hit. "Oh my god, is that what's been underneath all this? That I just feel inadequate as a woman?"

Now the tears came, of immense sadness, of relief. They were streaming down her face, in this crowded restaurant, but she didn't care.

Matt reached for her hand and held it to his lips. "Dear, sweet Nicole. Nothing could be further from the truth."

She just sat looking at him, seeing him seeing her, all the way down to her soul. His eyes told her how much he honored her, cared about her, valued her. There was a deep knowing she'd been truly *seen*, that there was no longer any use pretending there was anything about her that was unworthy of him because it was right there, in his eyes. It was a moment she'd been seeking all her life; she knew that now. It filled her, completely and forever. In less than the blink of an eye, her life had changed.

This sensitive, precious man had given her a gift from his heart so profound there were no words pure enough to thank him. So she just sputtered. Somehow, he understood.

"Sam loves you. You know that, right?"

She nodded, trying desperately now to wipe away the wetness covering her cheeks.

"And there was a time not long after you met when you were boyfriend/girlfriend for a while, right?" Again, she nodded.

"Well, during that time did he ever act like he'd stopped loving you?"

"No, he was really happy. I was the one who pulled away."

"And even after that, you pulling away, he has continued to love you, right?"

"Yeah." She looked a bit sheepish now.

"Well, don't you think this guy has paid his dues? I mean, what more could you want? I saw the way he looked at you when we were rafting, watched him take care of you even though I was there. That guy loves you more than anything in the world. And even though you keep him at a distance, he still thinks you're enough, still hangs in there with you. Sam seriously deserves a chance, don't you think?"

She had to admit, he did. It boggled her mind how much he had put up with all these years. She'd given him her love, then abruptly pulled it back and stuffed it down. Sam deserved so much more. He deserved more from her. Suddenly she felt horribly ashamed, and she dropped her head into her hands. Matt could see where she'd gone and gently chided her.

"Now, don't fall into feeling bad about how you've been with him. That's futile, and water under the bridge. Just make it up to him. Remember that on the raft, when you had a choice of my hand or his, something in you chose him. I think you're still in love with him, Nicole."

He lifted her chin, and the smile on his face brightened hers. She smiled back.

"God, you're incredible, Matt. I will try." She looked deeply into his blue eyes and reached for his hand. "We both have our work cut out for us, don't we?"

He sighed. "That we do."

As he thought about Amanda, and she thought about Sam, they both tightened their grip on the other's hand. The phrase "holding on for dear life" came to Nicole's mind.

"Ready to lighten things up a bit?"

"You bet. How about a deep breath and another drink?"

They called the waitress over and ordered another round, then chatted some more about the events of the day. Especially all they'd seen in the museums. History being Matt's favorite thing, he'd seen much to talk about. Nicole was fascinated by how observant he'd been, how he'd put all the new information together with what he'd read about the Wild West before. He had a grasp of the period that made it come alive for her as he spoke.

The drinks and the conversation relaxed them, put them in a party mood. It was almost ten when they got in the car to head home.

Remembering how they'd held each others' hands so tightly after talking about Sam and Amanda, Nicole wondered—what would happen next for them?

chapter 27

In stark contrast to the laughter and easy chatter in the restaurant, silence was the atmosphere on the drive back to Nicole's. Both of them knew something had shifted in their relationship. Even once they got inside the house, they were quiet. Neither of them was sure what to say.

Finally, Nicole broke the uneasy spell and said, "Matt, tell me if I'm wrong, but I'm feeling like there's been an energetic separation that's happened with us."

He nodded in relief that she'd had the courage to name it first.

She continued, "I've always known you belong with Amanda. And now you're telling me I should really give Sam a chance." She made a funny face, as in "yeah, you found me out." "So what I'm sensing is that it's time for our physical connection to be over."

There, the words were out. Both knew it was true, but as the weight of it sunk in, the sadness did too. Their intimate times together had been healing and exhilarating.

"Nicole, you know how much I care about you..."

"Yes, I know, Matt. I care deeply for you too. How could I not? My connection to you goes soul deep, and it will always be there. Yet our paths are separate."

"Thank you for understanding. Seems like you're one step ahead, all the time. You're extraordinary."

"So are you, Matt, and I can't pretend it's not kind of sad that I don't get to have that delicious body of yours again."

Matt blushed, then laughed. "Back at you, Nicole."

They looked at each other, both wrestling with the next question. This time Matt spoke first.

"What do you want to do about tonight then?"

Nicole closed her eyes to better feel into what was the best thing to do. When she opened them, she said softly, "I honestly don't know if I could sleep tonight if you weren't by my side. To have you in a separate bed would just be too much of a ripping apart."

Matt nodded slowly. "What if we sleep in your bed but maybe with T-shirts on, to tamper the temptation?"

They smiled with the realization that one or both might indeed crumble without some barrier, no matter how small.

"You know that sounds good to me. Shall we?" Nicole took his hand and led him to the bedroom.

After quick bathroom visits, where they each changed clothes, they crawled in bed and stared at the ceiling. Matt reached for her hand, kissed it tenderly, and that is how they spent their last night together—side by side, holding hands.

chapter 28

Nicole opened her eyes to the familiar sight of her bedroom, then, as sensations from her body started to register, she realized she still held Matt's hand. She turned to look at him. His head was turned toward her, and she studied every feature of him, knowing this would be the last time they would be so close.

When he'd told her he'd had to book an early flight back to San Diego, she'd been disappointed they wouldn't have the day to spend together. But with the turn of events last evening, she was grateful. To spend much more time with him, when they'd already energetically separated, would have been excruciating. It reminded her of when she was in the waiting room at the veterinarian's office, holding her beloved but terminally ill cat one last time before having her put down to end her pain. Knowing what's about to happen turns even the bliss of being together into a desperate longing for it to be over. The letting go can't really happen until they're gone.

She watched as he slowly awakened, and his eyes met hers. His mouth widened in a sad, sweet smile that melted her heart. She was so going to miss that smile.

"Good morning, dear one," he said.

"Good morning to you too, Matt. Thank you for being here with me. Sleeping with you like this was, well, perfect."

"It was. It really couldn't have been any other way. I'll remember our last night forever." He reached out to stroke her cheek, softly, slowly.

Nicole could feel the tears welling, sadness overcoming her as she realized how little time they had before he would disappear from her life, so she turned her head to kiss his hand, then sat up. Looking at the clock to get her feelings in check, she said, "We'd better get a move on."

"Yeah, you're right," he murmured. His emotions were in turmoil. The pull of Amanda was strong, but in this moment he couldn't fathom severing the special and deep connection with Nicole. He didn't want to leave her bed, to leave her, but he knew it was time. Reluctantly, he got up.

They took turns in the shower, made coffee and got ready to leave in near silence. Nicole watched him surreptitiously as he moved about her house, taking in every detail of his body—the one she would never have again. She let herself remember what it was like to run her hand down his chest, kiss his soft yet firmly sensual lips, play with his hair and have his strong arms around her. Tears welled again when she thought of how it felt to have him inside her, and she had to stop. She forced herself to bring back the happiness at knowing he was going home to his true love, Amanda.

Matt too was torn. His future, he hoped, would be with Amanda. His heart thrilled just thinking he might have a chance with her now. Yet there was no way to deny the feelings he had for Nicole. His instant hit at the campground—*I have to know her*—had been spot on. They'd formed a connection so intimate, so profoundly important to his growth, that it was next to impossible to leave. It left him uncertain what to do or say to this dear woman, so he said nothing.

Finally, just before they left the house, he pulled her close, held her tight. She collapsed in his arms, holding the moment, then ever so gently pushed him away.

They tried to be casual on the ride to the airport. She told him about several good restaurants in the terminal where he could get a real breakfast before his flight. He talked about how much fun he'd had on the rafting trip. They knew they were just filling space, but there was nothing left to do. When they reached the drop off, it was all Nicole could do to get out of the car.

With his bag on the ground beside him, Matt turned to her. The sadness in his eyes was unmistakable and his shoulders sagged. Nicole spoke what they both were feeling.

"So once more we say goodbye." She choked up, and Matt reached out to pull her hair from her face and gently kissed her on the cheek.

"You're so special to me, Nicole."

"And you are to me, Matt." She tried hard to hold her feelings in check—no time to cry now. With a long, slow breath, she managed to get it out. "I hope things go well with Amanda. You deserve to get her back."

"Thanks, Nicole. And I hope you and Sam can get it together." He shuffled with his bag and gave her a melancholy smile. He longed to hug her close again. He knew if he did, it would make the separation that much harder. "Guess I should be going."

She gave one last look into those blue eyes she loved so much. "Yeah. Bye, Matt." She attempted a caring smile.

"Bye." He dropped his head and stepped back slowly.

She watched him as he walked to the terminal door, waited to see if he'd turn around, ready to give him a wave. He didn't.

Unable to move for a minute, it took prompting from a security guard to get her in the car and heading home. Tears streamed down her cheeks. She couldn't have said why—was it losing Matt? But she knew he belonged to Amanda, had known it from almost the beginning. And she was well aware that people often enter another's life just to provide an experience or lesson—a temporary connection, however profound. Or was it what he'd said about Sam, how she should give him a chance? Jeez, how did she feel about Sam? The feelings swirled around in her like a hurricane, releasing in huge, heavy sobs.

How was she ever going to sort this all out?

chapter 29

With Matt gone, again, Nicole doubled down on the wedding plans for Hayley and Mark. She'd received several texts from Hayley over the last few days about the flowers. Apparently, now the original plan of pink and lavender wasn't working for her. Now she wanted pink, yellow and white as the theme, which kind of threw off the rest of the plan with the chairs, which would now have pink and yellow roses tied to the backs with white ribbon bows that trailed to the floor. This meant rethinking a number of details, including the table centerpieces. Sam would come over in a bit so she could bounce a few ideas off him.

As soon as he walked in the door, face set and eyes downcast, Nicole knew they wouldn't be doing any work today. Without even saying hello, she jumped up and poured them both big mugs of coffee. Sam had followed her into the kitchen and flopped onto one of the bar stools. She handed him the coffee and waited for him to begin.

"Well, how was your weekend with Matt?" His eyes flashed with pain and anger, and Nicole found herself resenting that he would—as he had so often before—push her to tell him about things she really wanted to keep private, things that belonged just between her and Matt.

"It was good." *Maybe he'll just let it go at that. Maybe... Oh, no, I know that look.*

"Can't you give me a little more than that? How many times..."

Her icy gaze made him stop. "I mean, did you finish your 'unfinished business'?"

"I think so. I mean, it goes in layers, so there's always another one to deal with. It's pretty much up to him now."

His puzzled expression nearly made her burst out laughing. That was obviously not what he'd expected to hear. She sipped her coffee while he tried to figure out what to say next.

"Um, what's up to him now?"

"Look, Sam, we're the best of friends, and normally I tell you pretty much everything. But the 'business' is Matt's business, things going on with him, and I can't share it with you. Please just drop it. Did we have sex? Yes, you know we did. Is this some kind of 'relationship' that will continue? No, that's not in the cards. He wants to go back to his ex-wife. Would I have wanted it to continue, were that not the case? I honestly don't know."

She paused to catch her breath, gave a melancholy sigh, and Sam reached out to touch her hand.

"I'm sorry, Nicole."

He wasn't entirely sure whether he was sorry she and Matt wouldn't continue, for her sake, or if he was sorry that he might have pushed her too far. *Oh well, either way...*

She decided to give him a detail to help ease his pain. "Last night, we just slept together, side by side, T-shirts on, holding hands. Doubt I'll be seeing him again."

Crap. She's not happy about that. She likes him more than she's letting on. This killed any joy he'd felt when she'd said that last sentence. *How can I be glad when she's sad? But how can I be sad when I should be glad? Jeez, is there any way out of this tornado?* This dilemma pretty much summed up everything, his relationship with this woman he loved so completely. Sweet torture—he'd read that phrase somewhere. Didn't feel so sweet right now. He stood up.

"Nicole, I don't think I'm in the best frame of mind to do wedding stuff. I'll call you later."

She nodded slowly, and he left her alone with her own pain.

It didn't take long for Nicole's tears to start flowing. For the umpteenth time, she'd thrust a dagger into the heart of her "teddy bear," the man who loved her so unconditionally. For the life of her, she couldn't understand why he put up with it all.

Impulsively, she put her hands together and held them high. *Please, please let me love him too. I want to love him again.*

chapter 30

God, what a dreadfully painful lecture. How was it even possible to make something as historically and morally important as the Civil War sound boring? *This will be my "do not do it this way" benchmark once I start teaching.*

Matt walked to the pub near campus to catch up with Mike and Charlie, his buddies from his first stint in college. Both had graduated in the usual time, but as they worked nearby, they continued to have lunch in the place they'd frequented as students—marginal food, but cheap—on Thursdays. As they waited to order, Matt vented his frustration with the professor. Charlie chimed in, having had the same guy at one point. There was plenty to complain about and reminisce about, and it kept them going through most of their meal.

Suddenly there was a loud clatter and the sound of a few choice curse words as a young waitress dropped her tray and its contents onto the floor five feet behind Mike. All three men watched her pick up the ruins of someone's lunch. She was wearing a short shift dress that rode up the back of her slender thighs when she bent over, almost, but not quite, to her crotch.

"Whoa, wouldn't I love to poke that," Charlie said with a lascivious grin.

"Maybe after I'm done," added Mike.

Matt clenched his jaw and narrowed his eyes. Just because they were men didn't mean they had to be jerks, and he was tired of it. That woman was somebody's daughter, maybe someone's girlfriend. Regardless of that, a human being who deserved to be treated with respect, just like that woman in Iraq. In a flash, his eyes widened in horror, his face rigid with pain. Distantly he could hear voices asking—hey you all right man?—but the sound didn't fully register in his brain. Finally, he remembered to breathe, and current reality came into focus.

"Dude, what happened?" Charlie shook his arm.

Matt turned to look at him, and his eyes went steely hard. It took a minute before he could find the words.

"Listen, I know it's guy talk, used to do it myself. Until…Do you really not get how disrespectful it is? And that it matters when we talk that way? It's not just harmless banter. It hurts people."

Mike and Charlie were stunned. A dozen expressions flitted across their faces, bouncing from one to the other like ping pong balls. Shock. Anger. Betrayal. Guilt. Indignation. Back to anger again.

Defensively, Charlie said, "Yeah, well, who died and made you Pope?"

Matt said tartly, "So maybe this is just my thing, but I'm not comfortable with that kind of talk anymore."

Mike turned to Charlie, then to Matt, uncertain of which way this was going. Finally, he said, "You know Charlie, it's always made me uncomfortable too, even though I say stuff. I feel kind of shitty afterwards." He glanced at Charlie to see how he was taking it.

Charlie shrugged. "Fine. I'll speak more 'genteel' around you wusses from now on." He rolled his eyes. "I gotta get going anyhow."

Mike stood up with him, said something about getting back to the grindstone, but Matt's mind was already elsewhere, and he didn't even wave goodbye as they left.

My god, it was like Iraq all over again, only in miniature. This time he'd actually spoken up. He hadn't frozen. He'd acted. Maybe even stopped two friends from talking like that again. It hardly made up for Iraq, nothing could, but man, this was some kind of progress.

chapter
31

Hayley was all smiles as she and Mark walked through Nicole's front door. Sam, always the jokester, had been hamming it up the whole drive from the airport to her house.

"Sam was singing along to country songs in this crazy, way less than perfect English accent." Hayley giggled. "It was hilarious."

Man, this guy really knows how to get clients to have fun while they're working plans out. There could hardly be a better partner, Nicole thought.

She had iced teas waiting for them on a tray in the living room. They all chatted about the concert Mark had played in Denver the night before as they settled into their chairs. Hayley looked so cute in her tight blue jeans and fringed blouse that Mark could hardly keep his eyes off her. *It's so cool to see how in love they are.*

Nicole ran through the general flow of the ceremony first, starting with Hayley's grand entrance in the carriage. "Can it be white horses please?" she asked. Sam assured her they could be any color she wanted, except blue. Mark chuckled.

Through detailed descriptions of the chair setup and altar arch, Nicole painted them a picture of what the ceremony itself would look like. When she got to the part about the vows, Mark took Hayley's hand and raised it to his lips. She kissed his cheek, then turned to Nicole.

"We've been working on our vows, but we're not quite done yet."

"It's actually harder than it seems like it would be, isn't it? To say just the right thing to the one you love, pick the perfect words to express how you feel."

Hayley nodded. "It really is. There's so much I want to say to him, but it would take an hour."

Mark smiled. "All good I hope."

"Well, most of it." Hayley teased, and everyone grinned.

Nicole went through the after-ceremony things like throwing the bouquet and the cake cutting, then went on to discuss the decorations in the reception hall. She showed them pictures of her idea for the centerpieces, which were mostly greenery with some yellow roses, pink peonies and white orchids strategically placed to give the feeling of casual flair. Hayley loved them but wondered if something sparkly could be incorporated too. Nicole made notes, said she'd see what they might come up with.

They'd pretty well gotten the flowers down; next up was music. The word was hardly out of Nicole's mouth when the mood changed. Apparently, Hayley and Mark had discussed this already and they were not in agreement, not even close.

Mark narrowed his eyes. "How can we abandon the country music that got us where we are, Hayley? It just wouldn't be right."

"But I want something more sophisticated for a wedding.

Songs about beer and trucks would cheapen the whole event. This is an important day, and it deserves important music."

"Important music?" Mark was livid now, almost shouting. "As in, country music is trash? Low class? Jeez, Hayley, why don't you just push that knife in a little deeper?"

Hayley crossed her arms and spat back, "You know what I mean, Mark. I'm country too, you know. For crying out loud I'm from *Tennessee*, you know like *Nashville*. You don't get more *country* than that."

"Oh and *Texas* isn't country? Get off your high horse, Hayley. You're such a snob."

Oh man, we're about to lose them. Think of something, anything, quick. To Nicole's immense relief, Sam broke in and calmly said, "Maybe there's a way you can both get what you want."

The couple whipped their heads around, anger not yet gone but a sliver of hope beginning to show on tense faces. Hayley spoke first. "How could that be?"

Sam's voice was respectful and soothing. "Well, what if the actual ceremony was more traditional, like a classical quartet. Then the reception, and dancing, could be country?"

Hayley brightened. "So I could walk down the aisle to something softer, then we could all-out party later?" She took Mark's hand and looked at him questioningly.

"Yeah, I guess that could work," he muttered. Then as he thought about it, his face turned to excitement. He kissed Hayley on the cheek and added, "I think I know who we could get to play at the reception..."

And once again they were off and running with ideas. Nicole had the names of a quartet in town who'd done weddings for their clients before. She promised to make arrangements for Hayley and Mark to hear them the next time they came out. Then, while the others chatted away about the band Mark had in mind, she reflected briefly on how Sam had handled the fight. *He's so good at smoothing things out. Instead of getting caught up in people's conflict like I do sometimes, he just finds a way to make it work. Without ruffling any feathers. Wow. If I were writing wedding vows to him I'd definitely have to say something about this.* She blanched as the idea of vows fully sank in. Quickly she coughed to cover the shock.

It was about time for Hayley and Mark to catch their plane back to L.A. Mark had a concert there the next day, and Hayley was doing promotional talk shows. While they were gathering papers and magazines to leave, Nicole spelled out what everyone's homework would be until they met again.

"Hayley, you need to work on the guest list. And start looking for your dress..."

"Ooh, I saw one in here somewhere." She glanced at the stack of magazines. "It had beaded lace in this really intricate design of swirls and radiating lines, like this." She drew imaginary lines on the table with her fingers. "I'll find out who the designer is and give them a call."

"Don't forget to look for your bridesmaids too."

"I have a couple ideas about them already, but I need to check and see if they'll like them. I don't want to be one of those brides who puts her bridesmaids in dresses they hate."

"Good for you. Mark, you need to arrange for the band and figure out what you want in the way of tuxedos."

"Okay, we're going with the gray thing, right?"

"Yes, medium gray. And start looking at wedding bands too,

something that will look good with that gorgeous engagement ring."

"Sam, you're going to continue working on the main menu—going with the venison, buffalo steaks, filet mignon et cetera as the main course."

"I can't wait to taste what delicious creations you'll make for us next time we get together," Hayley said.

Nicole continued, "I'll line up the quartet, and keep working on the thousand and one decoration details still to do."

Happy with how the meeting had gone, they said their good-byes. Nicole gave Sam a grateful wink as he walked out the door. He grinned and made a gesture as though tipping a hat to her.

Adorable.

chapter 32

After Sam left with Hayley and Mark, Nicole poured herself a glass of wine, intending to start on the details that were her homework. But she couldn't concentrate on the wedding; all she could think about was Sam. Sam, and his calm demeanor. Sam, and his gentle smile. Sam, who brought everything into perspective and found solutions where there hadn't seemed to be any. And Sam, who loved her with all his heart.

He was an amazing person, she knew. Kind, strong, loyal, fun, a bit of a perfectionist when it came to his culinary creations, but so yielding to her in other areas. Their communication had been easy and deep from the beginning. There was little they couldn't talk through with each other. Their connection was so solid. But for the lack of physical intimacy, they might as well have been married. She had such respect for him, cherished his presence in her life. She shook her head as she realized how empty it would feel if he weren't in it.

And he was definitely sexy, she had to admit. Remembering the times they'd made love stirred her in ways she hadn't let herself feel for a long time. Whether hot and intense, or the slow tender lovemaking he preferred, the love had always been heartfully expressed, physically, emotionally and energetically. He'd been so fully present, with her. Why had she pushed that away?

As she reflected, Matt's words came back, loud and clear, "You belong with Sam." Oh, god, she knew he was right, had known it all along. "You need to let that man in." She took a big swig of her wine, for courage, and decided to have another pass at this. Why was she still shutting him out? Where had this belief that she wouldn't be good enough for a man to want to stay with her come from? That little girl inside, the one who could only cry, was the key somehow. Was she feeling unlovable? Was that it?

Nicole decided to get back in touch with her. She closed her eyes and took several deep, slow breaths. *Now see the stage, empty. Bring the little girl out.*

Oh, there she was, sitting in a little white chair, center stage, in a white dress with a pink silk sash. Scared as all get out, being by herself. At first, Nicole just watched her, her fidgeting, her total discomfort at being alone. God, she was so afraid, and Nicole's heart ached for her. Nicole could feel how this child had no resources to deal with grown-up life, no abilities to handle what might be asked of her in an adult relationship. How she could hardly *give* love; she needed, desperately, for love to be given to her. She needed protection, and comfort, and guidance—safety. Suddenly Nicole felt herself on the stage, kneeling in front of the little girl, the little girl who was such a part of her. She grabbed her, holding her close, tears streaming down her face, and said, "I will love you, even if no one else will, and we will love each other, always." The little girl cried and hugged her back, clinging to Nicole for dear life. They held each other tightly, heart to heart, for a long time. Nicole felt the healing taking place, a deep, profound healing of the soul.

Then suddenly she was back in the room, her home, now. Without a doubt, a radical shift in her had occurred. She could still feel its effects—the terror and helplessness the little girl had felt was gone. In fact, it seemed to Nicole that she had left the stage and was no longer even there trying to be in control of something that was beyond her capabilities. The stage was clear for a more mature piece of herself to step in, even though none had yet. She sat for a long time, just letting it settle, feeling the peace. Shifts of this nature had happened to her before, and she knew it was yet to be determined how her outer life might reflect the change. Sometimes it had been immediate; sometimes the unfolding took many months. *Patience, it will be revealed.* For now, she just needed to believe it, not let it go.

When Sam returned from the airport, he quickly realized Nicole was in a radically different space than when he'd left. She didn't move to hug him as she usually did, and when he said "hi," she didn't even look him in the eye.

Okay, something's weird here. She's acting almost bashful. What the H is that about? What happened after I left? Oh shit, did Matt call again? I don't think I could take another round of that...

Nicole caught the look on Sam's face—the hard set to his jaw, the flash of hurt in his eyes. The same look he'd had whenever they'd spoken about Matt. She gave him a quick, pleading look.

He just caught the end of it, and watched her blush and turn away.

That didn't seem like it had anything to do with Matt. Is she being shy with me? Has something changed in how she feels about me? Oh, please, please let that be it.

She needed to keep him from asking her questions, so she took a deep breath and steadied her voice.

"Ready to get started on the final menu?"

Back to business as usual, huh. I wish she would just tell me what's going on with her. She knows I can see it. Why won't she tell me? Crap, should I ask her?

She looked him in the eye just as he was about to speak. Her expression told him in no uncertain terms that she needed space now.

"Sure, Nicole. I think we're set on the appetizers and main course. I just don't have a final decision from Hayley about the side dishes."

He poured himself some coffee, and they continued to discuss the wedding plans. Every once in a while, he would catch her studying him, questions in her eyes. She would quickly look away before he could say anything—so unlike her.

"By the way, Sam, I was really impressed by how you handled their disagreement about the music. For a minute there, I was kind of worried they might actually call off the wedding. Thanks for saving the day."

"No problem, Nicole. It was such a simple solution, I wonder that they didn't see it themselves." He smiled.

She watched as he carried his coffee cup to the sink. *I have to tell him, about the shift. And I want to. But I can't yet. I have to hold this energy, keep it close. If I tell him about the little girl, about the healing, too soon, the energy could dissipate. It has to keep working, internally, for now. As much as I wish it could take me back to him, I don't know where my soul wants this to go. It would kill him, kill us, if I jumped the gun here...*

"So Sam. I think maybe we're done here for now. Could you send the menu to Hayley?"

Oh. This isn't going to happen now. She's not ready. Again, I have to go back to waiting.

Still, when he stood up to leave, he brushed her hair back from her face and gave her a long, tender kiss on the cheek.

chapter 33

Matt picked up his phone, that marvelous contraption that could connect him once again to the woman he loved. Or blow it completely if he said the wrong things to her. "Courage," he heard Nicole say, "courage." He pictured the wonderful woman he'd met camping, felt how compassionate and accepting she'd been, brought back the energy and understanding of their conversations. He took in three deep breaths as she had once instructed him to do, and punched in the numbers he knew so well.

"Hello."

"Amanda, this is Matt." He tried desperately to keep the apprehension out of his voice.

"Oh, uh, hi."

"Is this, maybe, a decent time to talk a bit?"

He could hear the hesitation in her voice as she answered. "Yeah, I guess so. What's up?"

"Well...there's actually a lot I want to say to you. Things I couldn't tell you before. And I'm so sorry, that I couldn't tell you when you kept asking. You deserved better, Amanda. It was just so hard...Anyway, something's happened to me in the last couple months, and I really want to share it with you. If you're still interested. I mean, if you've totally moved on, and don't care anymore, then just say so. I still love you, never stopped." He hadn't meant to bombard her like that, but once the words started they just kept rolling. He waited breathlessly for her response.

"Matt..." She felt that deep aching for him. She'd never stopped loving him either but was also afraid of being sucked back into that horrible hole of *no connection* that had been their relationship ever since he'd returned from Iraq.

"Is there any chance we could just get together and talk?"

She wanted to, she really did. They'd meant so very much to each other, and now he was offering the very thing she had wanted from him. Her heart told her to take the chance.

"Okay."

"Oh, God, Amanda, thank you." The relief in his voice was immense, and he didn't try to hide it. "Are you free for lunch Thursday?"

"Yes, where?"

"Daniel's, eleven-thirty. Does that work for you?" Daniel's had been a favorite place of theirs all through the college years. He was so hoping just being there again could bring back a little of the feelings, before Iraq had screwed it all up.

"Okay, see you then."

"Until Thursday, Amanda."

His heart was racing. She still cared, at least enough to hear him out. But the things he had to tell her. How could he ever explain it as well as Nicole had?

A totally outlandish thought hit him. Maybe Nicole should be there too.

chapter 34

Nicole was so absorbed in pictures of flower arrangements for Hayley's wedding that she picked up her phone without looking at the name on the screen.

"Hello?"

"Well, I know this is getting to be a bit ridiculous, me popping into your life yet again."

Oh my God, Matt. Her heart did a somersault and landed somewhere south.

"Dude, you know I love hearing from you. How are you?"

"Mostly okay I guess. Yet to be determined, actually."

"Which means…?"

"I talked to Amanda."

"Matt that's so great! How did it go?"

He let out a jagged breath. "Actually, all that's happened so far is that we set up a time to talk. Lunch on Thursday. And…" The word hung in the air between them as he gathered his courage. "I have a really big favor to ask."

"Sure, Matt, anything."

"You might have to take that back when I tell you what it is."

Okay this is going to be major. She steeled herself. "Just spit it out, and we'll see where it goes."

"I want you to help me talk to her."

Shock hit her in waves so hard she actually dropped the phone. *What, WHAT!!?* She stared at the little metal and glass object, the one that had just relayed those preposterous words, as though it had bitten her. Finally, she picked it up.

"Criminy, Matt, are you sure? That could go horribly wrong really fast. Have you even told her about me?"

"No, not yet. We haven't talked about much at all yet, just set up the lunch."

"Jeez, Matt you can't just spring me on her. She'll…"

He quickly broke in. "I won't. I was thinking that maybe if you were here in San Diego, and you were standing by, so to speak—then at the right time we could all three talk."

"Why on earth do you want *me* there? Won't telling her about Iraq and the dreams be hard enough for her?"

"Yes, I know that. But Nicole, I'll never be able to explain all the things you taught me, what you showed me, the way you could. I don't think I understand it well enough to get it through to her, and I certainly couldn't answer questions like you could. I'd put you up at a hotel, to make it less awkward." He paused expectantly.

She so wanted to help him with this, she really did. But this could be a disaster just waiting to happen. Too many variables: would Amanda even agree to talk with Nicole there, would she even be able to *hear* what Nicole would say, or would she just tune Nicole out and turn to hating Matt? This could end Matt's chance with Amanda forever, and she wasn't sure she wanted to have a hand in that.

If it went well though…

"I'll do it. Well, I think I can. There's a lot going on right now with this wedding Sam and I are planning, and I have to be sure he can carry the load while I'm gone. Let me check."

The relief in Matt's voice was palpable. "Oh, Nicole, I can't thank you enough. Really. From the bottom of my heart."

"It's not a done deal yet. I have to talk with Sam, find plane tickets and get a prescription for valium…" She laughed.

He chuckled. "Man, I thought you were serious there for a second."

"As if."

"So I'll find you a hotel here, maybe Thursday through Saturday? Let me know if that works with your flights?"

"Okay. I'll get on it here. And send you flight info when I get it. You know, it will be good to see you again."

"It will, Nicole. You're really the best friend I've ever had."

"I love you too, Matt. Get back to you later."

Her heart pounding, eyes open wide with apprehension, Nicole fought to get her emotions under control.

Holy cow, where is this man taking me now?

chapter 35

As soon as she could, Nicole called Sam and asked if they could do lunch. That was a pretty normal thing for her to do, so he didn't even think to ask her why. Then with her head reeling, full of excitement about seeing Matt again and worry about how Amanda might react, she looked online for the best way to get to San Diego. It took some time. This was short notice, but she finally found something that would work and not break the bank. Well, Matt's bank, as he had said he would reimburse her for the tickets.

She met Sam at the brewpub they liked best. It was a friendly atmosphere, in the neighborhood hangout sort of way. The whole place was centered around the wrap-around bar. Booths lined the walls, and the upper level was glass so patrons could watch the brewers while they worked. They'd spent many a night here laughing and drinking with friends.

After they ordered their usual club salad for her, Reuben sandwich for him, Nicole began.

"So, how's the menu coming along for Hayley?"

"Great. I think we're almost done getting it just the way she wants. Man, that woman is so picky, but I have to admit she's got excellent taste. This is going to be a kick-ass reception."

"I'm really glad to hear that, because I don't want to leave you high and dry, but I need to go out of town this weekend."

Sam looked at her blankly. "Uh, why?"

She paused, knowing he wasn't going to like what she had to say next. "Matt called." Sam's face fell. "He needs help with something, and I told him I'd come to San Diego."

"What could he need your help with?" he asked, though he was afraid he might already know. She'd told him enough about the camping trip to guess the worst, the close bond they'd formed.

"I can't tell you. I know that sounds shitty to say that to you, my wonderful friend. But some secrets are just not mine to tell."

Clearly upset, his eyes flashed with anger and pain. "Well, crap, Nicole. Just go. I'll handle everything till you get back."

"Sam, you know I wouldn't leave if it wasn't really important. Matt is a friend..."

He twirled a French fry around in the ketchup, wanted to smash it into the plate.

"Yeah, I know about this *friend*. Let's just drop it." *As I have a million times before, every time you choose to be with someone else instead of me...*

He bit his lip and withdrew into the relative safety of talking about work. "How's your end coming? The flowers and bridesmaid dresses?"

She decided to let it drop and followed his lead.

"Well, Hayley really likes the pink and yellow thing we've already talked about, and she wanted something sparkly, so I'm thinking glitter on the evergreen sprigs, and maybe some..."

They continued to discuss the wedding plans while they ate and slipped into the easy casual way of being they'd enjoyed for so many years now. She looked at him from time to time, wondering how it would be if she really let him in, as Matt had told her she should. The shift with the little girl had been profound, and she knew it would change things at some point. But apparently not yet. She could still feel an internal hesitation...

She paid for the meal, the least she could do, considering.

"Thank you, Sam, for carrying the load for a while. And understanding." She knew he needed more from her in this moment, but she had to focus on Matt and Amanda, and the coming conversation that could change their lives forever.

"Yeah, well," he scoffed and looked down at his feet.

"I'll call you when I get back."

She'd already turned around and was walking away, so she didn't see Sam's eyes mournfully following her as she went down the street.

chapter 36

Nicole's flight was late.

"Oh, Matt, I'm so sorry," she said as she hugged him hello. "Are you sure you have time to get me to the hotel before you meet Amanda?"

"Yes, just. If we hurry. It's good you didn't check luggage."

"Yeah, it is."

Matt put her carry-on in the back seat and opened the door for Nicole.

"And thank you so much for coming. I can't tell you what this means to me. I'm so nervous about all this."

Matt stopped talking to concentrate on getting out of the airport mess. Once they were on the road, he continued.

"You know, just seeing you again is making me feel more hopeful. I think if I can just get Amanda to meet with you, we'll be okay."

She started. "Jeez, Matt. I have to admit that worries me a bit. It almost sounds like you're depending on me to *fix this*. And I don't have that kind of superpower. This really needs to be mostly up to the two of you."

"Nicole, I'm sorry. That really came out wrong. A much better way to have said that would be that with you there to support me, I think I can get through to her."

Nicole relaxed, put her hand on his arm. "Okay. Honestly, all either of us can do is get it all out for her, give her everything she needs to make a decision. Then it's going to be up to her."

"Don't I know it." His expressions flipped from fear to hope and back again with lightning speed. He gave Nicole a grim smile.

"Matt, it really is a good sign that she's even going to meet with you. She wouldn't do that unless she still cared about you."

Matt pulled into the hotel entrance.

"I do know that. Guess I needed to be reminded." He smiled weakly.

Nicole hopped out of the car as soon as it came to a stop.

"Hang in there, Matt. And let me know how it goes."

"I will."

Matt held up crossed fingers, then drove away.

chapter 37

There she was, just as beautiful as the day he'd first seen her in that college classroom. In spite of the apprehensive look on her face at the prospect of hearing what Matt might have to say, she still took his breath away. His love was still strong, even after all the years and the trials they'd been through.

"Amanda, thank you so much for meeting me. Uh, can I hug you?"

"Yes," she said and opened her arms to hold him. She'd been afraid it would feel weird, considering, but really it felt like home.

They sat down in the booth they'd been in so many times before. When the waitress came around, they ordered drinks and said they needed more time before ordering food.

Matt took a deep breath and began. "Amanda, I have hated being away from you. And I have hated not being able to share with you, well, everything. I want to, now. You deserve to understand. But a lot of it will be difficult for you to hear, and I guess I need to know that you won't just walk out in the middle of it. I'm not trying to scare you. I'm just trying to say that if you did, you would never know the whole truth, and that really would be the end of us. Do you understand what I'm saying?"

"Jesus, Matt, this sounds heavy. How am I supposed to know if I can stick it out, when I have no idea what you're going to say?"

"Please, Amanda. Look at me. I love you with all my heart, and I'm willing to bare my soul to you. The things I need to tell you are very unpleasant—I know that. I've been living with them for a long time now, basically living in shame. But that's changed, and there actually is a light at the end of the tunnel for me, for us, if you can let it in."

She looked searchingly into his eyes, the eyes she'd always thought she could look into forever. And there was the Matt she'd known before, the loving man she'd married. She no longer saw the haunted man who'd come back from Iraq so broken and closed. So she took a long breath and said, "Okay, I'll listen, and I won't run."

The waitress came around just then with their drinks, and they let her know they wanted to talk for a while. Recognizing the intent looks on their faces, she told them to wave her over when they wanted her.

Matt took a deep, steady breath, told himself to stay calm. "It started with a camping trip I took. Beautiful spot in the mountains. Would you believe Wyoming? I went there to be alone, and think—about what I was doing with my life, about you."

He chewed his lip, gathering up the courage he needed for what he had to say next.

"In the campsite next to mine was a woman. No way was

I looking to get involved with another woman, but from the moment I saw her, something pulled me to her. She just had this energy that made me want to talk to her. And I know you're not going to want to hear this, but yes, we had sex."

He could see the flash of pure anger in her eyes, the look that said how could you do that with her when you wouldn't with me. So, softly, he said, "Please, let me explain all of it before you kill me."

She hissed, "Fuck you, Matt," but she didn't move.

"I had talked to her for a little while the first night I arrived. And the next day it just kind of happened. She was dancing, and I joined her and well…Honestly, it was a total surprise to me. Even I was asking myself—how come her and not you? Amanda, I think it was because she had this energy of acceptance about her. Like things would be okay. When we talked, it just felt like I didn't need to be afraid of her reactions. It's really hard to explain. That night—yes, I'm sorry, we were sleeping together—I had one of my nightmares. And she was so gentle, asking me to tell her about it. So I did. I told her. Something in me trusted that she would know what to do with it all. And she did. She's very wise, Amanda, in a way that no one I've ever met before is. She helped me see what happened to me in Iraq, and the nightmares, in such a different way."

The look of anguish in her eyes made him stop. He reached for her hand, but she pulled it back.

"I know it hurts you to hear this. And God, I hate to hurt you. But it's the only way to get the whole truth to you. Nicole is the one who broke through to me, not because she meant more to me. Nothing could be further from the truth. But because she has this way of seeing things differently, this compassion, that I needed.

And I actually think it helped that I don't have strong feelings for her, love feelings. My feeling for her is mostly just huge gratitude."

"Yeah, well, how does she feel about you?" Amanda was still seething about how close Matt had been with Nicole. Unbidden images of the two of them together kept flashing through her mind, and she felt hot and angry, and cold and sick all at the same time. *I should just get out of here now. Isn't there something I need to clean at home? Maybe tackle those boxes in the garage? Anything would be better than this.*

"Like I said, compassion. She had a bad marriage early on and is seriously not interested in being too close to anyone again."

Amanda relaxed, just a bit.

"So now will you tell me about Iraq, and your dreams, and why you wouldn't make love to me when you got back?"

"Yes. I will." He swallowed hard. "I do have another request though. I would like to have Nicole be part of the conversation." The look in Amanda's eyes almost made *him* want to run.

"Are you fucking kidding me? You want me to meet with some woman you screwed? I can't even tell you how much I hate you right now." Every muscle in her body was clenched in anger. He'd never seen her so mad. Tears sprang to his eyes. They tugged at Amanda's heart.

"I know, believe me, I know. Please don't go, Amanda. The one and only reason I'm asking this is because I'll never be able to explain some of the things I need to tell you as well as she can. She's the one who really understands the new perspectives she taught me. I barely get it, and it has turned my life around. If you could hear what she told me, it could turn *us* around too."

He reached out to her but stopped short of touching. No way she would allow that now. "I want that more than anything."

"I don't know if I can do this, Matt. I need to think..." She looked at him mournfully. "I have to go."

"Please, will you call me? Nicole is in town at a hotel for the next two days. She's here just to help me explain all this to you. But she has to go home after that, and I don't know if she'd be willing to come back later. Please..." He was begging now.

She looked beat. He couldn't tell from her expression if she was really considering this, or just wanting to get away.

"I'll call," she finally said, the tone of her voice unreadable.

Matt watched her walk out the door and wondered with a sinking heart if he'd ever see her again.

chapter 38

While Matt and Amanda met, Nicole had decided to check out the Modern Art Museum. Turned out to be a good thing to do—wander around looking at stuff without having to really think about it. Because, of course, her mind was riveted on what might be taking place with Matt.

Had Amanda stayed long enough for Matt to say what he wanted so much to say to her? Had she been able to understand any of it? How much had he tried to tell her? Nicole knew that not many people had ever thought about things the way she did, the way Matt could now see it. Even his grasp of the concepts she'd introduced him to was tentative. Why else would he have asked her to come?

What if Amanda just bolted and wouldn't let Matt finish what he needed to say? Declared it to be over, completely? This whole trip would be for naught. All her work with Matt would be for naught. Well, not really. It would kill him to lose Amanda, but he could love again, she was sure. Such a tender, giving soul would not be alone for long. Would he come back to her? She shook her head, startling a young man standing nearby. No, she wouldn't go there. He belonged with Amanda.

Then she tried to imagine how it would be to actually talk to Amanda. God, that poor woman would have to be so torn up over losing Matt, then having to hear about Iraq and his dreams. And to have to see this new woman in his life. Nicole knew she probably couldn't stand it, to be in Amanda's situation.

Around and around in her head, the thoughts spun. Finally—amazing how you can forget when you're caught up in something—she remembered to sit still and get centered. She sat down on a bench, closed her eyes, cleared her mind of the busyness. Open again, the gentle knowing that there were much larger forces at play here, in a delicate dance of souls, brought her to a place of perfect-trust internal calm.

Her phone buzzed with a text from Matt.

> Well, she didn't run, but I don't know if she'll meet with you. She said she'd call. Can we talk, over dinner? Can I pick you up at six?

Nicole texted back:

> Sure, meet you in the lobby.

And now we wait, she thought.

Once Matt arrived, they decided to just have dinner in the hotel's restaurant. Online reviews said it was good, especially for seafood, which Nicole loved. Interesting that a girl who'd grown up in a land-locked city in cattle country was so hooked on lobster, shrimp, scallops and crab. It made her wonder about the past lives possibility.

They ordered dinner along with their drinks. Matt had not had lunch after Amanda left and was famished. He told Nicole about the conversation he and Amanda had started at Daniel's. Well he hoped it was just a start, that there would be more to come.

"It sounds to me like you said what needed to be said up to now, Matt. Even that was a lot for her to take in, so it doesn't surprise me she's having to think about it. God, I know I would."

"I can't disagree. But it's killing me, the waiting. Truly, my whole life is hanging in the balance here."

"So is hers, Matt. She said she'd call, and I believe she will. Just be patient."

Matt made an exasperated face and put his head in his hands. When he looked up again, he said, "Maybe we should talk about something else for a while."

"Good idea. Tell me about your classes. How are they going?"

They chatted then, about his school, the wedding plans she and Sam were working on—as much as she could tell him, considering who the clients were. When he asked about how things were going with Sam, Nicole stopped short.

"Honestly, Matt, I'm doing my best *not* to think about Sam right now. There's so much on the line for you and Amanda. I need to focus on that. This conversation between the three of us, if we have it, is going to be difficult."

"Don't I know it," Matt grimaced. "Speaking of difficult conversations…"

He told her about the incident with the bent-over waitress and his friends Mike and Charlie, how he'd spoken up about their disrespectful comments. She agreed he was making a lot of progress.

When they'd finished picking over their meals, and the waiter brought the check, which Matt picked up, she got serious again.

"You know, Matt, as much as I love being with you, I'm wondering if it would be better if we didn't spend much time together while I'm here. Two reasons. It's really not going to help for us to sit here churning on everything while we wait for Amanda's response. We'll just go crazy."

"Actually, I think I'm already there." Matt laughed.

"Right behind you." Nicole grinned. "Also, if she should ask if we're seeing each other while I'm in town, you really want to be able to tell her no, other than this dinner where we talked about her."

"That's a good point." The gratitude in his sweet, blue eyes warmed her heart. "You're always so thoughtful, Nicole."

"I'm just really wanting this all to work out for you two. You deserve it, Matt."

"Thanks for saying that. I hope she sees it that way. So what will you do while you're hanging out here?"

"Oh, there's lots of stuff to do here, as you know. And Sam made me bring work for the wedding."

Matt raised his eyebrows and grinned.

"No, silly, not ours. For the clients. Though I have been thinking about all the things you said…"

"Glad to hear it. I guess just let me know if you need some ideas of things to do." He sighed. "Maybe we should call it a night?"

"I think so. Let me know as soon as Amanda calls you. I'll be waiting on pins and needles."

"Will do, Nicole. Good night then." He got up and held his arms out to hug her.

She hugged him, a friend hug, said good night, and went up to her room alone.

chapter 39

Matt was shocked when he got a text from Amanda the next morning. It said simply: *Yes*. Relief washed through him. He loved her so much. Now there was hope. Quickly, he texted back *thank you*.

He arranged with Nicole to meet at Chancery Park that afternoon, and Amanda said that worked for her too. Then he bought a bottle of Amanda's favorite wine, grabbed a blanket, in case they couldn't find an empty table, and headed to the park.

Nicole would find her own way to the park. The last thing Amanda needed to see was the two of them arriving together. It would be hard enough having them in such close proximity as they talked. His mind leaped to the worst—an all-out catfight, kicking and screaming, then both of them beating up on him. He'd heard stories, seen the movies. So much could go wrong.

But it could also go very right. Meeting Nicole had turned the tide in his life. Why would that end now?

Matt was the first to arrive. Sure enough, all the tables were already taken. But he spotted a shady place under a big leafy tree that felt right. Closing his eyes, he said a silent prayer that things go well. Then he stood and waited for the two most important women in his life to join him.

Amanda walked up shortly after. Matt thanked her for coming, and they tried to make small talk, but it was too awkward. After a couple attempts, they just fell quiet.

Five minutes later, Nicole arrived, frazzled.

"I'm so sorry to be late. I gave the driver the wrong directions."

She briefly touched Matt on the arm—a hug would have been too much for Amanda—then held out her hand to Amanda.

"I am so thrilled to meet you. You're the love of this guy's life, you know, and now that I see you together, I can see why."

She's beautiful, Nicole thought. *The kind of beauty that permeates every cell of her.* Amanda's blond hair fell in long, soft curls to her shoulders, accentuating the large, gray eyes and delicate features of her face, as well as her petite figure. *She and Matt would make the most incredible children.*

Amanda was clearly surprised at Nicole's warm greeting. She hesitated, then shook Nicole's hand.

"Shall we sit down over there? I brought some wine to help us get started," Matt said.

As they walked to the tree, Amanda tried hard not to stare at Nicole, but she couldn't help it. Who was this woman who had done what she couldn't do—open Matt up, get him to talk, make love with her? The tears started when that thought hit. This woman knew her beloved Matt better than she did now.

Matt could see how upset Amanda was, and frightened really. He hated how hard this was for her. But truthfully, he was frightened too. If Amanda couldn't handle what was coming next, this might be the last time he'd ever see her. He spread out the blanket, and before they all sat down, he reached for Amanda's hand and raised it to his lips. When he looked up, she was crying. Nicole pulled a tissue out of her purse and handed it to Amanda.

"Thanks," she muttered.

Matt glanced at Nicole. She could see the turmoil in his eyes. She held his gaze steadily for a moment, lips in a small smile to say, *it's okay, Matt; it really is going to be okay.* Then she sat as far away from Matt as she could without seeming too obvious.

Matt poured the wine, handed a glass to each of them, and then said, "I don't know any other way to do this other than just plunging right in. Amanda, are you ready?"

She looked at Matt, then at Nicole. Amanda knew this would be hell, but it had to be done if she wanted this man in her life again. She nodded.

Matt told her first what had happened in Iraq, about the woman and his buddies, how he froze, his shame that he hadn't even tried to stop them. He told her of the unbidden thoughts that would come when he saw a woman bent over, or on her knees. Amanda's face went ashen as she listened, and Nicole quietly held a calm space for them. When Matt spoke the image of his nightmares, Amanda's expression turned to horror.

Nicole broke in at this point.

"Amanda, it's very important to remember that each person

has many different parts inside, many actors on his internal stage. All different ages, different genders even, and with different agendas, and ways of looking at life. For example, I actually ran into a piece of me, one time in meditation, who was a playboy and believed he could go out and 'sow his seed.' When I told him to look down—dude, there's no penis there—he was stupefied. He was so clueless, he didn't even realize the body he was in was female. I only bring this up because the piece of Matt that is reflected in his dreams is a very, very small part of him, one that is quite detached from the rest of him. It's not representative of who Matt is in the world. But of course, it's a real shock to come across a piece like this that feels so heinous. And it made him afraid of himself, ashamed of himself. He was scared to death that part would hurt you, if he made love to you."

Matt nodded his head at Nicole's words.

Amanda was silent a minute, trying to let Nicole's words in.

"I don't understand. If he has dreams about…that…" She couldn't say the words that described the awful dreams. "Then doesn't it mean he wants to do that? That he's capable of doing that?"

"Not necessarily. There's an energy there, yes, but its purpose may not be to act that out in life. At least that's what I believe about Matt."

She told Amanda her own story about the part of her who connected with the man who beat his kid to death. Amanda's eyes went wide hearing it, yet she listened attentively and seemed to be getting what Nicole was telling her.

"Well, if those horrible parts are there in both of you, but you say they won't act out in life, why are they there at all?"

"That's a really good question, Amanda. And I'm not at all

sure I have any answer. My little pea brain can't begin to fully understand what something as complex as the soul really wants, how all these funky pieces serve. But I do believe that they serve us somehow. For Matt, I think this piece actually came forward to help him deal with what he saw in Iraq, and remind him that those energies are in every man, deep, deep down."

Amanda looked at her in complete surprise. "You think every man has that in him?"

"Yes, to a certain extent. It's a primal force. It's not coming out of ego or surface consciousness, our minds as we know them. Which means it's not personal, it's not something that *belongs* to anyone. It's just an energy that might be expressed through them. Humans have a lot of those instinctual impulses that we especially needed when we had more primitive lives. Certainly doesn't mean every man would act it out, obviously. Very few do. And Matt is not one of them. Especially now. He's come to accept that he has that part inside. By accept, I do not mean he, or me either, think that raping a woman is in any way an okay thing to do. Believe me, I do not. I've been raped. I speak from experience." She glanced briefly at Matt. "Back when I was in college."

Matt was shocked. Nicole had not told him about this before. And Amanda suddenly had a new sense of this woman before her, a woman who had been through an experience she couldn't even imagine, and yet had been so kind to Matt. She felt a kinship with Nicole—in spite of, or because of, or, wow, she really didn't know—how close she and Matt had been. Tears of appreciation sprang to her eyes.

Nicole turned to Amanda with a look of profound admiration.

"I just have to say that I think you're amazingly brave, to be sitting here listening to all of this. And not just with Matt, but me too. Honestly, if I were in your position, I don't know if I could. You must love him very much, Amanda."

Amanda looked at Matt with tears still in her eyes and said, "Yes, I did. And I think I still do, but with all that's happened today, I'm really not sure of anything right now."

"I don't blame you," Matt said. "Believe me, I've been living with this for years, and I'm not sure of anything either, except that I still love you. Thanks to Nicole though, I do have a glimpse of possibility that gives me hope. I know this will be hard for you to hear." His face grew taut with anguish. "She taught me that who I am as a lover was not changed by the Iraq experience or the part of me that shows up in these awful dreams."

Amanda went crimson, and her mouth set in a hard line. The word "lover" hit her like a hard punch to the stomach. All her thoughts of the evening before came rushing back. Thoughts of Matt's mouth on Nicole's, his hands all over her body, their two bodies locked together, their cries of release. She wanted to lash out at both of them, but she turned her focus to Matt.

"How could you do this to me, to us? With her?" She spat the words out in rage, frustration and desperation.

But it was already done, and no words in the world could take it back. Again the tears came, and she dropped her head and let them flow.

Matt was in torment. He so wanted to reach out, to hold Amanda and tell her how much he loved her. But he knew he wasn't worthy of that yet.

"Amanda, when I came home, I was so filled with guilt and shame about what had happened over there. You were so pure and sweet—I just couldn't make you have that awful stuff in your head. I couldn't accept it all myself. How could I expect you to? So, I didn't say anything. It killed me to not share with you. I wanted to be the kind of man who doesn't keep secrets. You deserved to have that kind of man, but I couldn't be him then. Now I can. Now I can know I have that piece in me but also know it's not likely to come out. Now I can...be with a woman and not be afraid of what I might do. Being with Nicole was healing for me."

He stopped, not sure how to go on. Amanda's shoulders were shaking with her sobs, and it stabbed him to the core.

He put his hands over his heart. Oh, how he wanted to take her in his arms. "I'm all yours now, Amanda, if you can find it in your heart to love me again," Matt said.

They sat in silence, looking at each other, for a long time. When Amanda sighed and broke the gaze, Nicole said softly, "Do you have any more questions for me?"

Amanda shook her head. While the anger in her had subsided for the moment, she was still too filled with anguish and confusion to speak.

"Then I think I'll exit now, and leave the rest for you two." Nicole turned to Matt, who put his hands together and bowed his head, Namasté. Nicole did the same and walked away.

chapter 40

Matt and Amanda sat in silence for a long time, silence that became more awkward with every passing minute. Neither could think of what to say next, what to do next. A ball from one of the kids playing nearby rolled up onto the blanket and broke the spell. Matt threw it back, then said, "Are you okay?"

"Matt, I don't even know what I feel right now. I'm so, so pissed at you for…what you did with Nicole." Her eyes flashed hot with fury. "I don't know if I could ever recover from that. And all that stuff you threw at me—Iraq, and your dreams. It's too much. I don't even know what to do with it. I heard it all, I did, but I can't make sense of it."

Her shoulders sagged, unable to bear the weight of it.

"I think I just need to be alone now." Amanda didn't move. She felt rooted to this spot, this time, because something in her knew that if she later decided she couldn't deal with what had been said here today, she might never see Matt again. The thought saddened her horribly. Was this how it would end?

Suddenly, in a blinding panic, she bolted to her feet, glanced hurriedly at Matt for one last time, and ran.

Oh my God, I've lost her. His pain was unbearable. Defensively turning to anger, he lashed out at Nicole. *I wish I'd never met you. How could you have talked me into telling all this awful stuff to Amanda? You just used me. I really hate you now.*

But Nicole, of course, couldn't hear his unspoken words. She'd already left. And even as he thought them, he knew none of them were true.

He packed up the wine and the blanket and went home.

As much as she wanted to, Nicole didn't try to find out what had happened after she left. Her part had been played, and it was up to Matt and Amanda now. She went back to the hotel, ordered room service and holed up with movies until she fell asleep.

When she woke the next morning, she stared at her phone for a long time—no message from Matt. The not knowing what had happened between them was tearing her apart. Did they keep talking? Were they talking still? Or had Amanda run, leaving Matt broken? Did they just need space? Is that why Matt hadn't called?

Aargh, just shut up already and get the first plane home.

After a short search, she found a flight that left in three hours—just enough time to pack up and get to the airport. And wrestle with the temptation to call or text Matt.

She didn't touch her phone.

She ordered a ride and split.

The plane ride home was full of second-guessing, regret and trying to hold center, as well as trying to let go. When she landed and turned on her phone, there was a message from Matt.

Thank you, Nicole. It's done.

The finality of the sentence made her heart sink. She called Sam and asked him to come over and get drunk with her. She wanted to get drunk, to forget for a while, and she desperately needed her best friend.

chapter 41

Obviously, Sam wanted to know what had happened in San Diego. It was written all over his face as he walked in the door of Nicole's place. But the way she said, "hi" in such a dejected voice told him things had not gone well, at all.

He went straight to the kitchen to pour a couple of glasses of wine, handed one to Nicole. Then, uncertain of what she needed, he sat down on the comfy, green couch beside her, and simply said, "Want to talk about it?"

"Not really. I think Matt's last text—it's done—pretty much said it all."

He couldn't quite read her expression. There was more to it than just disappointment that one of her relationships had ended. He was all too familiar with what that face looked like. No, her face had hints of "I failed" and that didn't seem to just have to do with her and Matt. She'd told him before that there was unfinished business. His curiosity peaked. Maybe something had gone horribly wrong with that. He held his tongue though, for now, because he knew it wouldn't be good if he pushed her.

"I'm sorry to hear that." He said it as gently as he could and put an arm around her. Suddenly she buried her face in his chest and cried in deep, heaving sobs, certain she'd blown it for Matt and Amanda.

"Oh, Nicole." He stroked her hair and held her close, his best teddy bear hug. Instinctively he started rocking her slowly back and forth, just a little. She burrowed into him, seeking the comfort he so freely gave her. There was no escaping how much this man loved her, and for once, she let it in.

Finally, the sobs subsided, and she pulled away just enough so she could look into his worried, brown eyes.

"Thank you, Sam," she whispered. "Someday, I might be able to tell you about it, but not now."

He nodded and softly touched her cheek. He desperately wanted to kiss her, hold her more. She hadn't let him hold her that way for a very long time. Instead, knowing she needed to get her mind off of…whatever this was, he asked, "Shall we just watch a movie then?"

"Yes, I think so," she said as she let go of him and reached for the remote. "Pick us a comedy." She snuggled up to him again.

They stayed that way until the wee hours of the morning, when Nicole finally went off to bed. Reluctant to leave her completely alone, Sam slept on the couch, yearning for a day when she might invite him to her bed too.

In the morning, Nicole seemed more herself, so they made something to eat. Neither of them spoke about the night before; they just tried to slip into normalcy. When breakfast was done, Nicole took a shower while Sam cleaned up. His thoughts wandered to her visit with Matt and what had made her so upset. He wanted to understand, to help her, but he knew he didn't have enough facts to sort it all out. It was a relief when she reappeared, and he had to stop thinking about it.

They talked then, about the wedding cake, table decorations and flowers. Nicole noticed that Sam's voice was just a little lower, just a little softer than usual. His tenderness touched her deeply.

When they'd finished their work and Sam got up to leave, Nicole hugged him warmly, for a long time, and kissed him on the cheek. Barely able to look her in the eye, he knew he had to leave quickly before he did something he might regret later.

chapter 42

Nicole had just finished sending out the latest plans of the big wedding to Hayley when her phone rang. *Holy cow, it's Matt!* She had not expected to hear from him again, and after that first awful night home, two months ago, had forced herself to put him out of her mind in fact. There was such finality in the words from his text, *It's done,* that she'd felt the whole situation with Amanda was a failure of epic proportions. So much so that she'd been afraid to even reach out to him again.

"Well, hi," she said.

"Hello, Nicole. It's nice to hear your voice. How have you been?"

"Fine, everything's pretty normal here. How are you? And hopefully Amanda?"

"That's why I'm calling." She could practically hear him grinning on the other end of the line. "We're getting married, again!"

"Oh my God, Matt! That's so great! When?" Relief poured through her.

"On December fifth. And Nicole, we'd like you to come."

She had to take a deep breath, feeling the enormity of the invitation.

"Seriously? Are you sure? Is Amanda on board with this?"

"Actually, it was her idea. I was afraid to bring it up, but she did. Nicole, our whole relationship has turned around. We both know it was because of what you helped me see about Iraq and the dreams, which happen less and less, by the way. Amanda still doesn't like thinking about you and me making love, of course, but we've had many very long talks about, well, everything, and we are so close now."

"Matt, I can't tell you how truly ecstatic I am to know you two are together again. You so belong with her. I knew that from the moment you started talking about her. This is making my day. Honestly."

"I know. Sometimes I can hardly believe it myself."

There was a short pause as Nicole considered something.

"You know, I feel very honored that Amanda is okay with me coming. But I'd think it would still be hard for her to see me, considering...I'm wondering if it might be easier on her if I brought a 'boyfriend' to the wedding. Even though you and I both know I don't have one."

"Yeah, actually that would be nice. Might be easier to explain to family and friends too. Let people think I met a couple while I was camping rather than just a single woman."

"I was thinking maybe I could bring Sam. He's kind of a ham. He'd have no trouble doing a good job as a pretend boyfriend."

"Of course, Sam! He's a kick. Definitely bring him. I'm sorry to hear he's still not a real boyfriend though. And thanks Nicole, for thinking of that. You're such a kind woman…"

"Matt, I know you'll understand when I say this. I do love you."

"I love you too, Nicole." They both were silent for a minute, remembering.

Returning to the present, he said, "I'll send you the invitation soon."

"Great. Bye, Matt."

~

Matt hung up the phone, giddy with delight. He was getting married, again, to Amanda! And the wonderful woman who had helped him win her back was coming to the wedding! Could life get any better?

What a rollercoaster ride it had been. In awe, he reflected on all that had happened since he last saw Nicole.

Two weeks after she'd walked away from the talk in the park, he still hadn't heard from Amanda, without a doubt the longest weeks of his life. Being separated from her since the divorce had been awful enough, but at least during that time he'd been able to hold onto the hope that he could somehow get it together and win her back. When she'd bolted, he'd felt like his last chance was gone, and the pain was excruciating. He feared he'd lost, really lost, the one woman he wanted to share his life with.

But right in the middle of his British history class, his phone had buzzed with a text from her. As soon as he saw her name, he'd jumped up from his seat and run from the lecture hall, with a hundred shocked eyes following him out the door. The text said simply, "I'd like to talk," but it sent rays of bright sunshine bursting into every cell in his body. He hadn't waited a second to call her, and amazingly she'd answered after the first ring.

They'd agreed to meet at Daniel's again, and this time the conversation was more open on both sides. She'd told him about all the angst she'd been through after his return from Iraq—the disbelief that he wouldn't talk about anything, that he pushed her away physically. How she just couldn't understand why he didn't seem to trust her anymore, even started to believe it must be her that was the problem. And he'd apologized to her again and again, though that's not what she'd been asking for. She had just wanted to get everything out there, clear the air so they could move forward. They'd talked about Nicole and what she'd meant, and had not meant, to Matt. When it seemed they had said it all, she'd gazed shyly at him, eyes glistening with tears, and whispered, "I love you, Matt."

The fear, hope, anguish and longing had burst like a bubble then. With a voice full of his love, right there on the spot, he'd asked her to marry him again.

She'd not said yes then. While one connection had been reestablished, the physical connection had needed some serious repair. That was a process that had definitely taken time, and care. Their first time making love had been very difficult for both of them. His anxiety that she might fear him, or reject him was matched in intensity by her constant, unwelcome thoughts about how he'd been with Nicole. They'd worked it through, patiently, over many evenings, until they'd at last broken through the difficulties and emerged into the shared pleasure they'd had before Iraq.

Finally, six weeks after the conversation in the park, she'd consented to a wedding date. Surprisingly, he'd never had so much fun planning anything in his life.

Meanwhile, his relationship with his dad had improved as well. Matt still couldn't tell him everything, but he'd said enough to bring a certain degree of comfort between them. The upcoming marriage had helped too. His dad had been almost as excited by the news as Matt was. Well, not really, but close.

Matt's life was on track again, after such a long, dark struggle.

He felt blessed, and oh so grateful.

Matt and Amanda slid into the booth at San Miguel's, their preferred Mexican restaurant. Even as poor college students, they'd come here for special occasions. The food was always fresh and authentic, not like the Americanized eateries in the fancier parts of town. This was their kind of place.

"Okay, I called her, and she's coming."

Amanda took in the news with some trepidation. She definitely wanted Nicole there—there wouldn't even have been any chance of a wedding without her work with Matt—but the idea of having this woman who'd been so close to him be there on *their* day still had her a bit on edge. She really didn't want thoughts of them *together* flitting through her head as they said their vows.

Matt read her expression and pulled her close.

"And she's bringing Sam. You know the guy I told you about. Her best friend, who has loved her for forever. She wants to be sure she isn't seen as a single."

Amanda smiled, and her eyes misted. "She really is kind, to think of that, isn't she?"

"Yes, she is," Matt answered quietly, thinking of his talks with

Nicole. "She's an extraordinary person, Amanda. I was very lucky to meet her."

He kissed his soon-to-be-bride on the mouth, conveying all the love and passion in his heart.

"She brought me back to you, the absolute love of my life, the one I could never fully live without. You mean more to me than words can begin to express." He kissed her again.

"I love you too, Matt," she said, just as the waiter arrived.

chapter 43

Sam arrived at Jen's house with his arms full of grocery bags. Everyone was coming to celebrate Jen's oldest son, Jeremy's tenth birthday, and "Uncle Sam" was making his famous burgers for the party. While Nicole helped him unload the bags, she casually—she hoped—told him about having heard from Matt.

Sam froze.

"And what he wanted was for me to come to his wedding. He and Amanda sorted things out, and they're getting remarried." She kept her face bright as she said this.

His look of relief tugged at her heart. "That's good news, right?"

"Incredibly good news, Sam. I've always known Matt belonged with her. He loves her so much. It wasn't his idea to get divorced. Iraq kind of messed him up, and she couldn't handle it. Some of our discussions while we were camping helped him get over the shit he'd been through and finally talk it out with her."

Clearly, he hadn't liked hearing about that camping trip, but he didn't bring it up. His curiosity was piqued when she mentioned Iraq, and the talks she and Matt had had. Always before she'd said she couldn't tell him what those talks had been about—the "unfinished business" as she'd called it.

"I want you to come with me, Sam," she blurted out.

"You do?" he said incredulously. "Why?"

"Lots of reasons, but mostly to share it with you."

He had such a look of longing in his puppy dog eyes she didn't know whether to laugh or cry. Clearly, her invitation meant a lot to him.

"When is it?"

"December fifth. We could fly to San Diego Saturday morning, do the wedding that evening, then have some fun on Sunday. Then fly home after. What do you think?"

"Can't lie—seeing Matt again doesn't exactly sound like fun. But I guess if he's attached to someone other than you, I can handle it." His mood lightened, and he gave her a mischievous grin. "I've never been to San Diego, so that would be cool. So, yeah, I'll come with."

"Thank you, Sam." She breathed a sigh of relief, walked around the counter to give him a big hug, and was surprised by a sudden urge to kiss him, really kiss him full on the mouth. *What the…?* Quickly she broke the hug and went back to putting the hamburger buns on a platter.

Sam seemed not to notice and busied himself making the hamburger patties. He had a special seasoning, an old family recipe, which made his burgers particularly tender and delicious. Everyone loved them. Jen peeped in from the backyard where she'd been setting up the tables. When she saw Sam, she rushed in to give him a hug.

"Oh, Sam, I'm so glad you're here. I've been craving a burger all week." Jen ate mostly chicken and fish as a norm. Beef was a treat.

"Well, I'm just about ready to put them on the grill. First batch should be done in twenty or so. When do the kids arrive?"

"Any minute." She glanced out the front window. "Here come some of them now."

"How many in all?" Nicole asked.

"I think we'll have ten, including mine. One is a bit iffy. Something to do with family being in town. Should make for a relatively manageable group."

"Yeah, that sounds good. At least until they all get that sugar high, then it could get interesting."

Jen laughed. "Oh, don't I know it."

"So what would you like me to do, Jen?" Nicole asked.

Jen gave her instructions. There was a lot to be done—filling water guns, setting out the side dishes and condiments, filling paper cups with lemonade. Nicole loved doing this kind of stuff with her sister, for her sister's kids. They'd been close as sisters could be, well except for the usual sibling rivalry as youngsters. Having an older sister, by three years, had always been a comfort to Nicole. It was Jen who'd taught her how to apply makeup, how to ride a bike, and, most importantly, what to do with boys. When their parents decided to move to Arizona, Nicole had realized that as much as she loved them, her bond with Jen was the deepest in her family.

The backyard had been decorated to look like Jurassic Park. Nick had dinosaurs everywhere. Even the birthday cake was a lying-down T-Rex. *Jeremy's gonna love this*, she thought. He'd been obsessed with dinosaurs since he was three, and at this point knew far more about them than any of his teachers. Nicole's present to him was a Lego Jurassic World Indominus Rex Breakout building kit, which Jen had told her he didn't have yet.

The kids were well behaved all through the meal, and Sam's burgers were a hit. Jeremy beamed with all the attention he was getting. His friends, as all ten-year-old boys are, were certainly into the bathroom humor. Nicole heard more jokes about farting, peeing and butts than she'd ever wanted to hear in a lifetime. It sent them all into such delightful giggling though—how could anyone complain?

With cake and presents finally done, Nick announced it was time for the water fight. Jeremy's friend Aaron hadn't made it, after all, leaving only nine kids, and there were ten water pistols, for two teams of five. So Sam stepped in to make it even. Jen, Nick and Nicole scrambled furiously to keep the guns filled while ten screaming kids—yes, Sam too—chased, ambushed and soaked each other. It was hilarious to watch. Nicole couldn't believe how excited Sam was to be playing with the kids. *He'd be such a great father.*

As the time for parents to arrive drew close, Nick called a halt to the water games. Jen had already put out a stack of plush beach towels, and the kids all dried off as best they could. When everyone had left, including Sam—who had a potential new catering client to meet—they started the massive cleanup. *Good grief, the amount of trash a birthday party can generate,* Nicole marveled.

Nick was still outside, gathering up toys and presents, taking down decorations soaked by the water fight. It gave Nicole a chance to talk with Jen while they cleaned up food and dishes.

"I heard from Matt yesterday."

"Oh?" Jen's eyes widened in surprise.

"Yeah, he's getting married, to Amanda again. They've invited me to the wedding."

Jen stopped what she was doing and looked hard at Nicole. "So how do you feel about that? You really liked him, didn't you?"

"Actually, Jen, it's great news. I knew Matt and I were never going to be a long-term thing. He's really special, but…Sam's coming with me to the wedding."

Jen raised her eyebrows. "And how did that come about?"

"I asked him. Considering how close Matt and I were, I thought Amanda would be more comfortable if I had someone with me. And really I just wanted Sam to come. We have fun together."

She looked as though she were about to say something else, but stopped.

"And…" Jen prompted.

"Okay, Matt gave me such a lecture when he was here, about me giving Sam a chance. I guess I was kind of thinking that maybe a weekend away together might help me…I don't know…see things differently."

"Well, you know how I've always felt about Sam. He's wonderful for you. So I'm wishing you good luck." She gave her little sister a hug. "And be sure to tell Matt congratulations for me."

"I will." Nicole put the last of the dishes in the cabinet. "Anything else you want help with?"

"No, thanks. I think we've got it from here. I know you have to meet up with Sam about the catering thing. I really appreciate all the help."

"You're so welcome. Guess I'll be going then. Love you."

"Love you too, sis." Jen winked.

chapter 44

Sam picked Nicole up bright and early on the day of Matt's wedding. Nicole had always liked getting to the airport with plenty of time before a flight. It was exciting, being in the atmosphere of people coming and going to and from so many interesting places in the world. She loved to people watch. Sometimes Nicole made up elaborate stories about them—like what would happen if that young man with the beard and ponytail started chatting to the rather plump gray-haired lady with the permanent scowl? What might they talk about? Learn from each other?

Not this time though. She and Sam would just have time to catch some breakfast before boarding. They had much to discuss. Christmas wasn't far away, and they were working on several parties. During the meal, they figured out most of the menus for each, and who they'd contract with for serving and bartending.

Then once they were settled in their seats on board the

plane, they started on the decorations. Nicole had downloaded a number of ideas, things she'd seen in magazines and interior design websites. Together they went through what she had, and she scribbled notes. Then she typed everything up, planner style, while Sam read the airline magazine.

She paused when the flight attendants came around to serve them drinks and realized Sam had been rather quiet for a while. Nicole wondered what was going on in that head of his because it didn't look like he was thinking about Christmas parties. Finally, he let her know.

"So, are you ever going to tell me what that 'unfinished business' was with Matt?" He looked at her with an expression that said he wanted her to answer but was also afraid of what he might hear if she did.

She turned in her seat, put her hand on his arm and looked him straight in the eye.

"Sam, you know I tell you pretty much everything. I could probably count the number of secrets I have from you on one hand, and right now I can't even think what they'd be. But this isn't my secret to tell. It's Matt's. I've told you it has to do with his time in Iraq, and I just can't say more than that. I can't break his confidence, any more than I could break one of yours. Can you understand that?"

He slumped in his seat, and his look of dejection prompted her to tell him a little more.

"Okay, so we had some serious talks about what happened to him. I helped him see a new way to deal with it all. But some of what I told him was hard to grasp all at once. That's why he came back to Cheyenne, to hear it again. Then he asked me to go to San Diego to help explain it all to Amanda. Which was a bit awkward, by the way. She held up okay while we all talked, but then apparently she bolted. That's why I was so broken up when I got back. I thought I'd failed." She sighed. "Now, can you live with that?"

"Yeah, I guess so." He squirmed and shrugged his shoulders. "I've been trying to figure out why it bothers me so much that you won't tell me. Truth is I feel shut out, like you two have your own little special club. Crap, that sounds pathetic, doesn't it?"

"Look, Sam. You're seriously making too much of this. In the long run, it doesn't matter. Matt's marrying Amanda. I'm not even going to be in his life anymore. The 'unfinished business' is old news." She raised her eyebrows and pursed her lips. "Actually, you could say it's finished now. So please just let it go. I want to have fun on this trip."

Sam searched her face for more clues but found none. Pushing her further wasn't going to do any good. He caved, gave her an accepting smile, and said, "Me too." Then with a brighter expression, he said, "Want to go join the mile-high club?"

Nicole slapped him playfully on the arm. "You letch!"

chapter 45

Nicole, of course, had made all the arrangements for the hotel. It was the same one where the reception would be and one of the smaller but fashionable hotels near the wedding chapel. To save them both money, they'd decided to share a room with two queen beds and take turns in the bathroom. How hard could it be?

They got to the hotel around one with plenty of time to freshen up and get ready for the wedding. There was a glitch at check-in though, where it was discovered they'd been put in a room with one king-sized bed. The clerk apologized profusely, but there was nothing he could do as the hotel was booked solid with wedding guests. He arranged to have one night taken off the bill and showed them to their room.

Yep, sure enough, one king. They moved their suitcases inside, and both stared at the bed, which somehow felt like the elephant in the room. Neither wanted to talk about it though, so while Sam got ready to take a shower, Nicole sat at the desk and wondered how this was going to work.

It puzzled her why she even thought this could be a problem. They'd been friends forever, were quite comfortable with each other. They'd spent numerous nights camping together, in separate sleeping bags. And, even apart from the months they'd been "more than just friends," he'd stayed at her house and she at his many times when one of them had had too much wine to drive. Yet here it was, this strange feeling that if they shared a bed, *something might happen*. Wow, is that what she wanted now? After her talk with Matt, and the surprise urge to kiss Sam at the birthday party, might this really be the next step? The thought both agitated and excited her.

Sam stepped out of the bathroom just then, with a towel wrapped around him. Hotel towels being what they were, it didn't wrap much beyond just, so the opening left his right leg tantalizingly uncovered when he walked. His chest hair was dark and thick, and soft to touch, she remembered, his thigh firm and oh so near his most precious parts. The sight of him, so almost naked, sent tingles through her. Memories of their most intimate times flooded her mind, swelled her heart. She had to pretend to be looking for something in her bag to keep him from seeing her suddenly flushed face. *Jeez, how have I been so oblivious all these years how seriously hot he is?* Luckily, Sam started in with his usual teasing.

"Okay, we've got two hours left. Think you can get ready in that short amount of time?"

"Duh, I think so. Are you done in there?" she asked, waving her hand at the bathroom door.

"Yeah. Oh, wait, let me get my stuff out of your way."

Nicole gathered her toiletries and clothes, and shut the door behind her.

When he could hear the shower running, Sam sat down on the bed and ran his hand over its expanse. He sighed. *Okay, just a few minutes of wishful indulgence.* He let himself remember what it was like to make love with Nicole, to lie body to body in bed while they talked, kissed and cuddled. He thought about the sweet expressions of love on her face as they shared themselves with each other, as neither had before. Oh, God, he missed that. He felt the stirrings below as he thought about stroking her breasts, feeling her hands on him, moving inside her. He allowed himself to imagine that it could happen again tonight after the wedding. Would she let him hold her again, kiss her again? Matt was getting married, after all. He wasn't competition anymore, was he? Sam would give anything for another chance with Nicole.

So lost in the fantasy and the wish, he jumped when he realized the shower had stopped. Quickly, he got up and dressed.

When Nicole stepped out of the bathroom, each of them stared at the other. Nicole had chosen a dress of lavender draped fabric that was wrapped tightly across her bust to accentuate her curves, but not show too much skin. From her waist, it fell into a full skirt to her knees. She'd found shoes that nearly matched the color and had her hair up off her face in one of those random curl do's. Sam wore a gray suit, pale blue shirt, and a blue and purple tie in a swirly design. His gray, suede shoes completed the sophisticated but soft look. It hadn't been that long a time since Nicole had worn a nice dress, and since Sam had been in a nice suit and tie—they were event planners after all. Yet somehow, they were seeing each other with new eyes. *God, you're gorgeous,* flew through both their minds.

Finally, Sam managed to blurt out, "Nicole, you look stunning."

"You're not so bad yourself, Sam. I'd forgotten how well you clean up."

"Aw, shucks." He grabbed her and gave her a playful hug, couldn't help himself—he so needed to just *touch* her. "I'm ready for a drink, how about you? We could hang out downstairs till it's time to leave."

Nicole quickly said yes. The closeness of Sam's body, that *one king bed*, and her thoughts from earlier had her feeling on edge. The edge of what she wasn't sure, but she wanted to turn her mind to Matt and Amanda's wedding. She could think about the rest later.

chapter 46

The wedding chapel was just as Nicole had imagined it would be, knowing Matt. Small and in the old Spanish style, therefore now a historical landmark, it was nestled between tall modern office buildings that seemed to envelop it almost to the point of crushing it. Nicole and Sam arrived just in time and so took a seat in one of the back pews on the groom's side.

Matt and his groomsmen already stood at the altar in traditional black tuxes with peach ties and yellow rose boutonnieres. Nicole stared intently at Matt, how nervously happy he obviously was, and found herself strangely torn in her own feelings. It was impossible to see him without wanting to be close to him. So many memories of their time together camping, and at her place later. The deeply personal talks they'd had, the sharing of their very souls. Yet here he was, ready to be forever wed to another, the woman he really belonged to. She wished she could have one more moment with him, to tell him how much he'd meant to her. It wouldn't change anything—she had always known he was never going to be with her, and she wanted him to be happy with Amanda—but still, it was so very hard to separate. She had to fight back tears.

While Nicole was watching Matt, Sam surreptitiously watched Nicole. There was no denying she still had feelings for the groom, and it dampened the hope that had been building from the time they'd left Cheyenne. He sighed sadly—if only she could look at him the way she looked at Matt—and reached for her hand.

His touch broke her somewhat indulgent reminiscing. Turning to Sam, she smiled brightly and gave him a kiss on the cheek. Then they couldn't help themselves, being wedding planners. They chatted in hushed tones about the flowers, the ribbons streaming down the sides of the pews and the display of candles on the altar.

The music started, and all eyes turned to the back of the chapel. One by one, Amanda's bridesmaids, four in all, walked slowly down the aisle. In full-length, flowing dresses of light peach tulle wrapped tightly across the bodice in various styles, with little flowers of the same color accenting the waist or the shoulder, they fairly floated. They took their places at the altar, and everyone stood as the organist began the wedding march.

Amanda was truly a vision. Most of her shoulder-length, blond hair was swept up on the back of her head in a bird's nest bun with one tendril falling gracefully down the side of her slender neck. A tiara, of ivory pearls and tiny flowers woven in, elegantly framed her beaming face. Her dress had a fitted bodice of satin with an organza overlay of mini-flower appliqué, and delicate beading trails falling down a full skirt. The top line of the bodice just covered her bust in a sweetheart neckline, then made a graceful

V down her back. The overlay had three-quarter-length sleeves with delicate flowers spilling down the arms. She carried a bouquet of peach and ivory roses, peach gillyflower, yellow sweet pea, and white calla lilies, with long satin ribbons entwined in the greenery and swaying gently over the skirt. As she walked slowly down the aisle toward Matt, Nicole could see his eyes fill with tears even through his smile.

"Dearly beloved, we are gathered here..."

Sam glanced at Nicole from time to time during the preacher's words, trying to gauge the amount of attachment she might still have to the groom. But as Amanda began her vows, his attention quickly focused on the couple.

"Matt, you know I've loved you since the day we met. And I thought I'd lost you after Iraq. You had closed off, and I thought you would never let me in again. But after your camping trip, you came back to me. You were so vulnerable, utterly honest, sharing the deepest parts of yourself with me. Sharing even things you were afraid would turn me away for good. Instead, it expanded my love for you. Now there are no secrets. Now there is trust between us, at a level I'd never thought possible. Now I know we can make it through anything. Together, as one."

She put the ring on Matt's finger.

"Amanda, I've loved you since even before the day we met." He smiled at her, and she at him, remembering his clumsy attempt to ask her out. "And I am so grateful that you held out for me, even though I pushed you away. It was never because I'd stopped loving you. The hope that I might someday be with you again is what kept me going through those years we were apart. Thank you, my love. Thank you for believing in me, thank you for hearing me, for seeing me, all of me."

"I do see you, Matt. And I love you with all my heart," Amanda said as he put the ring on her finger.

Nicole bowed her head, overcome with emotion. She was deeply humbled. Such an honor it had been, to have played a part in bringing them back together. When at last she looked up again, her eyes were glistening, her face smiling.

Sam saw the smile, hoped against hope that she might finally have let Matt go.

"I now pronounce you husband and wife." The newly married couple didn't wait for the preacher to say "you may kiss the bride." Matt pulled Amanda close in a jubilant embrace, and they kissed passionately. The joy in the room erupted in applause and cheers.

Matt and Amanda made their way down the aisle, hand in hand, grinning from ear to ear. Twice they stopped to kiss again, which brought more cheers from everyone. Nicole glanced at Amanda's mom, who was crying with happiness in her husband's arms. Even Matt's dad had tears in his eyes. *The last few years must have been quite an ordeal for them too*, Nicole thought. *I'm so glad it turned out well in the end.*

At the entrance of the chapel, the bride and groom greeted each guest in the reception line. When Nicole and Sam reached them, Amanda took Nicole's hand first.

"We're truly happy you could come, Nicole." She gave her hand a friendly squeeze. "And this must be Sam," she said, turning to him.

"Yes, hi. So nice to meet you. Very moving ceremony and beautiful. You're a lucky man, Matt," Sam said, holding out his hand to shake Matt's.

"It's wonderful to see you again, Sam. So perfect that you could come with Nicole. I'm hoping you'll take good care of this woman."

Nicole blushed, but Sam immediately took the opportunity to put his arm around her waist and hold her close. "Oh, I certainly will," he said.

Matt took Nicole's hand, and they shook in the way casual acquaintances would. Well, it would look that way to an outside observer who didn't know. The tenderness of their touch and the deep connection when their eyes met said more to each other than any words could have. The moment was brief but complete.

"Congratulations to both of you," Nicole said warmly as she let go of Matt's hand. She glanced at the line of people waiting behind them. "We'll catch up with you later."

"You got it."

After Nicole and Sam had moved on, Amanda whispered in Matt's ear. "They really are a couple. She just doesn't know it yet."

"Yeah, that's what I told her. I'm glad you see it too."

chapter 47

The reception hall in the hotel was even more lavish than the wedding chapel. They'd just been college students when they married the first time, so the ceremony had been simple. This time, after all they'd been through, they wanted to celebrate to the hilt. They'd decorated in the peaches and yellows chosen by the bride, making the atmosphere decidedly cheery. Yellow and white balloons hung from the ceiling in a canopy that covered the entire room. There were vases filled with flowers—the same roses, lilies and sweet pea as the bridal bouquet—all along the front of the wedding families' table as well as on numerous pedestals around the room. Peach-colored starched napkins stood folded like tulips in wine glasses on tables set with gold-rimmed white china. Various sizes and shapes of glasses partially filled with sand on the bottom, with flowers and shells on top, served as centerpieces, along with taper candles in crystal holders.

Sam and Nicole found their places at a table near the back of the room and introduced themselves to the three other couples already seated there. They didn't have time to chat for long. Everyone cheered when Matt and Amanda, hand in hand, walked to the front of the room and sat down. When the rest of the family was seated as well, Mike, Matt's best man, stood up and loudly clinked his glass with a spoon.

"Good evening, ladies and gents. I'd like to take this opportunity to roast," he grinned at Matt, "er I mean toast, the happy couple." Amanda and Matt both cringed as Mike told stories of them in college—how they met, their first somewhat disastrous date and tales of their first wedding. He graciously skipped over the divorce and the unhappy period after. By the time he finished, most of the wedding party was in stitches.

The bridesmaids were a bit gentler with tales of Amanda, mostly telling stories of her love for Matt. When they'd finished the toasts, they teamed up with the groomsmen to sing a parody of Matt and Amanda's favorite song.

Just as Nicole whispered to Sam, "I'm starved. When are they going to let us eat?" Matt announced they'd be calling tables to go through the buffet line.

Sam was especially interested to see what would be served, considering he and Nicole had the wedding for Hayley and Mark to arrange, and their menu was not yet completely set. The buffet started with a slider bar of lobster rolls, crab salad sliders and lamb sliders, plus an assortment of various olives, cherry tomatoes and green salads. For those who preferred a heartier meal, there was prime rib, poached salmon, cheddar and jalapeño scalloped potatoes, and asparagus with lemon sauce.

"Hey, this is really good," Sam said to Nicole with the

asparagus sauce on the tip of his spoon. "Just a hint of mint. Think Hayley would like it?"

"Yeah, I do. It'll work well with the venison and buffalo. Can you figure out how to make it?"

Sam gave her an exasperated look. "Uh, yeah, I think I can."

Nicole poked him in the ribs, laughing. "Gottcha."

"Ooh," Sam suddenly grabbed her hand and pulled Nicole to her feet. "We have to dance to this one." The DJ had put on a song they'd loved when they first met—Luke Bryan's "Drunk on You."

Out on the dance floor, he twirled her around twice, then she fell into him, giggling.

"Dude, slow down."

He grinned and pulled her closer, wrapping her with his arms. Cheek to cheek they danced, bodies pressed together, swaying to the music. All Sam could think about was how perfect this felt—to have the woman he loved so much next to him, moving as one. With great intent, he willed his love for her to his hands, his fingertips, his body as he held her, wanting her to feel every bit of him. He moved his head just an inch and kissed her softly on the temple.

Nicole couldn't help but feel what Sam was doing—sending her all his love. The soft kiss, so sweetly given, the tender holding, his gentle presence guiding her across the floor. She felt his warmth, snuggled into him, inhaled the faintly smoky smell of his skin. Her breasts felt his chest; her fingers ached to run through his hair. Her body, with its wisdom unfiltered by the fears her mind had held for so long, responded to him fully. Her hips felt his, and the soft bulge of his crotch, and the potential of the king bed flashed strong through her mind. Amazingly, it was all so familiar, so exciting yet so perfectly comfortable being with her best friend in all the world. It felt like home. It felt good. It felt right. She wanted more.

They'd both been so focused on their dance, the sensual touch of each other's bodies, it took a while for their brains to register that the song had ended. And the one now playing was a much faster tempo. Embarrassed and somewhat reluctantly, they broke apart. Sam was too full of love and desire to look at Nicole. She was still reeling from her feelings of wanting to be intimate and couldn't let him see. So they danced awkwardly for a minute.

"Hey, want some more punch?" Sam tried to lighten things, get them back to some semblance of normal.

"Oh, yes, that would be great, Sam, thanks."

As Sam walked away toward the drink table, Nicole went back to their seats, sat down, and watched him intently. The glow from having been so close to him lingered, and her mind went back to the time they'd been even closer, the time they'd been more than just friends.

She couldn't deny that their first time making love had been very special. Sam had waited for months to get to that moment, and he wasn't about to rush it. He'd made her a light, delicious dinner, strewn candles all through his apartment. They'd talked about how they'd met, and he'd stroked her hand, her cheek, touching lightly during the meal. When his lips met hers, they were tender and wanting, and she responded in kind. They'd explored each other's bodies slowly, patiently, letting the pleasure and desire build. When he'd finally entered her, he'd cried.

Though most of their lovemaking was as tender, not every time had been like that. Sometimes their passions had taken them over in the most unlikely of places, and they were lucky they hadn't been caught. Still, what she most remembered now was the expression he'd always had after—that look of immense love for her, his happiness to be with her. And if she filtered out the irrational fear she'd had of not being enough to hold him, she could almost admit that those had been the best three months of her life.

For the briefest moment, she allowed herself to fully feel the love she had for him, and in a sudden flash of insight, she realized that was the true reason she'd never fallen in love with anyone else, including Matt. She was still in love with Sam.

"Here you go." Sam handed her a cup, then saw the look of nostalgic contemplation on her face. "What?"

"Oh, nothing," she said, flustered. "Just flashing back on the past for a second."

Great, we have a nice dance, and she goes straight to thinking about Matt. Damn. Why can't I just leave this woman behind? Oh, yeah...

Nicole saw the crestfallen look on Sam's face and was just about to say something when there was a ding ding ding on a crystal wine glass. The best man was announcing the cutting of the cake.

Matt and Amanda stood next to a three-tier, beautifully decorated wedding cake with peach icing roses cascading down and across the layers. Sam guessed it had buttercream frosting and made a mental note. Nicole looked at Sam, and they could tell each was thinking how great this style could be for Hayley and Mark's cake. With different colors, of course.

The bride and groom each took hold of the pearl-handled knife, engraved with their names and date, and cut off a slice. Amanda placed it carefully on the white china plate, cut off a bite and gracefully smashed it into Matt's mouth. Laughing, he stepped back and wiped the cake that hadn't made it into his mouth off onto the floor. Then he cut off a piece for her, one with plenty of icing. He gave her a look that said, "I love you, wife," and slowly moved the cake to her mouth. But just as she was about to take it in, he quickly smeared icing all over her nose. Pretending to be shocked, she pouted, and then gave him a kiss that spread icing over both their faces. The crowd cheered.

After the laughter died down, Amanda's mother handed them towels to wipe off the cake, and servers cut pieces for guests. Matt gave the signal to the DJ to queue up the "first dance" music, and everyone made way on the floor for the bride and groom. They started with a waltz.

Nicole and Sam were amazed to see how gracefully Matt guided Amanda through the moves. Obviously, they'd had some lessons and enjoyed dancing this way. It warmed Nicole's heart to see how tenderly Matt held his new bride. Then the waltz faded, and "No One Like You" by Scorpions came on. They had put together a choreographed dance for this one too, and again the crowd cheered, watching how in sync they were.

Seeing Matt dancing, hips moving in that sexy way he had, took Nicole back to the intensity of their time in the camper. In the blink of an eye, her emotions flew from longing to dance with him again, to sadness that could never happen, to gratitude he had been in her life at all, to joy at seeing someone she cared about being so happy with the one he loved. Inwardly, she sighed.

Then she turned to Sam and smiled, took his hand in hers, and they watched together.

chapter 48

Sam and Nicole had just filled their punch cups again when Matt walked up to them.

"Mind if I have this dance?" he asked.

"Sure," Nicole said as Matt whisked her away. Sam was left standing with the two cups and didn't look at all pleased about it.

They made certain not to get too close while they danced. High school prom chaperones would have been proud. Neither of them wanted anyone, especially Amanda, to be at all suspicious there was anything other than a casual friendship between them.

"That was an amazingly beautiful ceremony, Matt. The vows—you obviously wrote them yourselves. Have to tell you, hearing them brought tears to my eyes. I'm so happy for you and Amanda I can't even say."

"It really was cool, wasn't it? I was so nervous. I had to practice and practice. I was so afraid I'd break down before I got through them. I think you know why." His face was set in a "normal" pose, but his eyes betrayed the intensity of the feelings coursing through him.

"I do, Matt. I could tell Amanda was really touched by what you said. Blows me away *she* didn't start crying."

Matt laughed. Sam and Amanda danced close by, and he said, "Doesn't Amanda look incredible?"

"She certainly does," Nicole said, looking right at Amanda. "She's the perfect vision of a bride who's very much in love."

Amanda blushed, happily. "Thank you," she said as Sam danced her farther away.

"So you and Sam are going back tomorrow?"

"Yes, we've got another event to get started on. A big corporate team-building thing. Long weekend in February. Not my favorite kind of job, but it sure pays the rent."

"Well, I can't tell you how happy it's made me to have you here. Especially since it would never have happened without you. Honestly, Nicole, both of us are so grateful. I still hardly know how you did it, the healing."

"I have to say, it was pretty tough, being with you, talking with you." She grinned, and he smiled back. Oh, she was going to miss that boyish grin.

"Yeah, that was tough. So has there been any progress with Sam? Sorry, I've been so caught up with Amanda that I haven't even asked…"

"I have been working on it, Matt. Talk about healing. The 'something' you tried really knocked me into a different space around relationship. I'm just not fully there yet."

"Well, I hope you make it cause I'd love to see you and Sam be as happy as Amanda and I are." Matt gave her as caring a look as he dared in the circumstances.

"That would be nice."

Suddenly, the energy shifted as both of them realized it was truly time to say goodbye, to move on with their separate lives.

"Listen, Matt. You know how much I care about you, as a friend. A very precious friend. And I'm here for you if you should ever need me. But I don't think you do now, and maybe it would just be best if our paths went their own ways." She looked deep into his eyes and could see that he knew the truth of what she was saying.

"Nicole, you know I feel the same way. I will always cherish the time we had together."

The song ended, and their hands dropped away from each other. Her voice full of tenderness, she whispered quietly, "I'm kissing you on the cheek," and walked away.

Nicole was still so caught up in the emotions of having said goodbye to Matt for the final time that she started when she heard a voice behind her.

"Nicole?"

She turned around to see Amanda standing beside her, alone.

"Hi, Amanda." She began the usual spiel about what a beautiful wedding it was and how pretty the flowers were, but Amanda stopped her mid-sentence.

"Please, can we talk for a minute? I need to thank you, for… everything. Matt was so closed when he came back from Iraq, and I couldn't open him up. You did, and I'm forever grateful. It was your…work that brought him back to me. Bless you." Tears welled up in her eyes. She had to lower her head to hide them from the crowd of people around them.

"Oh, Amanda, you're so welcome. He loves you deeply. I knew that the minute he started talking about you. Honestly, it fills my heart to see you together now." She put her hand over her heart. "And I have to thank *you*, because watching you two gives me hope that I might finally be able to open myself to having the kind of relationship you have."

"What about Sam, Nicole? Matt's told me how much he loves you. I could see it too, when you were dancing together a few minutes ago. And unless my eyes were deceiving me, you looked pretty happy, being in his arms." She gave Nicole a quizzical sideways glance.

"God, Amanda. I know. Matt talked to me, well scolded me really, about Sam. He helped me a lot with some issues I have around being able to let Sam in. I'm not there yet, but...getting closer I guess."

"Well, that's encouraging, Nicole."

Nicole nodded.

They stood in silence for a moment, reflecting on what an amazing mystery human relationships can be, and how their lives had become so intimately entwined, if only for this short time. They smiled at each other, full of appreciation and gratitude. "I guess it's all worked out pretty well."

"It did indeed, Nicole, and I know you'll find what you're looking for." She glanced briefly at Sam, who was standing not far away. "I hope you have a wonderful life."

Nicole almost reached out to hug her but thought better of it. Instead, she offered her hand to shake Amanda's and said, "And I wish all the very best for you and Matt."

With a heartfelt smile and a look of finality, Amanda let go of Nicole's hand and rejoined the wedding party.

chapter 49

Matt and Amanda were about to leave the reception hall for their honeymoon when one of the bridesmaids, not too gently, reminded Amanda that she hadn't yet thrown the wedding bouquet. So Matt shouted for all the single ladies to gather, and about a dozen did. Nicole and Sam were standing near the back. She wasn't particularly into this ritual and assumed Amanda would toss it to one of her bridesmaids. There was a bit of jostling on the front row. Clearly, there were several women determined to be the one to catch the prize.

Amanda looked over the expectant crowd, focused her eyes on Nicole and threw the bouquet directly at her. There was nothing for Nicole to do but catch it, and she did. Her first reaction was to look sheepishly at Amanda, but then she realized what this dear, sweet bride had done for her—a handing of the torch—and she bowed her head to her, tears quickly coming to her eyes.

Everything Matt had said that last evening in Cheyenne came rushing back. His surprise "proposal" that plunged her into the depths of what had been holding her back from truly opening to relationship. Those beliefs that she could never be "enough" to hold onto a man. The proof that it wasn't true, in the form of the dear man standing next to her now. And her sudden realization after their dance that she was still in love with him.

In a holographic instant, she felt Sam's body so full of want as he pressed her against the wall after the Cheyenne Frontier Days meeting, felt that hot flush of desire at the sight of Sam's barely covered thigh in the hotel room with the one king bed, saw Sam waiting for her as she walked with her bouquet down the aisle on their wedding day.

Sam had his arm around her waist as he often did when they were together. Nicole usually felt it as a casual touch, but suddenly she felt it in a new and precious way, as intimately as their dance earlier. With the bouquet still in one hand, she turned to face him, looked at him lovingly, with full intent. He saw, felt, the shift in her, said *I love you too* with his soft brown eyes, and smiled shyly.

Suddenly serenely confident in their future together, she threw her arms around his neck, holding her body tightly to his so there could be no doubt, and kissed him passionately.

When finally she remembered they were still surrounded by people, she broke away and whispered breathlessly, "I think we need to go upstairs."

Flooded with desire, and surprise, he grabbed her hand and led her out of the room. They waited for the elevator in silence, each afraid to break the spell. He breathed a sigh of relief when the door opened, and he knew they were going to be alone.

As the door closed, Sam gently put his hand on the back of Nicole's head and pressed her to the wall with his body, just as he had that day at Cheyenne Frontier Days. She moaned, and pulled him to her tightly, her tongue caressing his. When the elevator reached their floor, they stumbled to their room, still not speaking.

Once inside, they undressed each other hurriedly. Moving to the bed, Sam's intent was to take it slow. He didn't want to somehow frighten her away again. But she pushed him onto the bed and climbed on top of him, wanting him *now*. They made love passionately, urgently. Years of denial and desire erupted into a desperation to be one at last. All his yearning, all his waiting, all his hopes—finally fulfilled. He cried out her name as they came together.

She collapsed onto him, fondling his chest hair as her breathing steadied. He stroked her back, still unable to speak. They lay there, together, in union, feeling the enormity of the transformation in their relationship.

But this wasn't the end of his wanting, or hers. Looking intently into her eyes, Sam rolled them over and began gently rocking them again, in and out, together and almost apart. He caressed her face, her breasts, conveying his love for her and his joy at their closeness. She responded with soft kisses on his face, his chest. Her whole body knew his, remembered how to move with him, how to meld with him. As the waves of pleasure built in her, she grabbed his hips, pulling him in deeper, harder, until the intensity burst in them both.

They lay side by side, gasping for breath, holding each other close. It was Nicole who finally broke the silence.

"I love you, Sam," she whispered.

He so wanted to believe her. But a cloud passed over his face as he remembered the nostalgic look she'd had after their dance.

"Are you sure? That 'flashback' you had earlier tells me you still have feelings for Matt."

She started back in surprise, then laughed gently. "Oh, Sam. You thought that was about Matt? I was thinking of you—how perfect and wonderful it felt to be dancing so intimately with my best friend. How happy I really was while we were more than just friends. How the reason I've never fallen in love with anyone all these years, including Matt, is because I still loved you. I love you, Sam, truly. I'm so sorry I pushed you away for so long, so sorry for all the pain I've caused you."

She kissed him tenderly and then held his gaze for a long time, until he could let it in.

"Thank you, Nicole, for saying that. I'm not going to deny it's been hard. Especially watching you with others." He grimaced. "But if you're really here now, really with me now, it was all worth it." Sam's expression grew intent as he added, "You were worth the wait."

He paused to let her feel the full import of his last sentence.

Then, finally expressing the desire that had been in his heart since he met her, Sam lifted her left hand to his lips and kissed her ring finger. "Marry me, Nicole."

And with a smile on her lips, and no trace of the fear she would not be good enough to hold him, she said softly, "Yes."

Acknowledgments

There are many people to acknowledge for their contributions to this book.

My wonderful mother, Elneta, my sisters, Jackie and Janet, and husband, William, gave me such insightful feedback as my first readers. Thank you so much for your support. And thanks also to my friends Gail, Bonnie and Julia who helped me as well.

I so appreciate Andrea Costantine and Polly Letofsky at My Word Publishing, whose guidance has been invaluable. Kirsten Jensen, my editor, I cannot thank you enough for your honesty and direction during the editing journey.

To my dear sister Janet Hamilton, who graciously offered to paint the stunning picture for the cover, I send my deepest gratitude.

My thanks go to Clare, who made me believe in myself.

And I'm immensely grateful to my husband, William, who walks the path with me.